1/07

The Day My Mother Left

The Day My Mother Left

By
James Prosek

simon & schuster books for young readers

new york london toronto sydney

SIMON & SCHUSTER BOOKS FOR YOUNG READERS • An imprint of Simon & Schuster Children's Publishing Division • 1230 Avenue of the Americas, New York, New York 10020 • This book is a work of fiction. Any references to historical events, real people, or real locales are used fictitiously. Other names, characters, places, and incidents are products of the author's imagination, and any resemblance to actual events or locales or persons, living or dead, is entirely coincidental. • Copyright © 2006 by James Prosek • All rights reserved, including the right of reproduction in whole or in part in any form. • SIMON & SCHUSTER BOOKS FOR YOUNG READERS is a trademark of Simon & Schuster, Inc. • Book design by Christopher Grassi and Lizzy Bromley • The text for this book is set in Sabon MT. • The illustrations for this book are etchings made by James Prosek on copper plates and printed by Anthony Kirk at the Center for Contemporary Printmaking, Norwalk, Connecticut. Etchings courtesy of Waqas Wajahat LLC • Manufactured in the United States of America • 10 9 8 7 6 5 4 3 2 1 • Library of Congress Cataloging-in-Publication Data • Prosek, James, 1975– • The day my mother left / by James Prosek.—1st ed. • p. cm. • Summary: When his mother leaves to live with another man, nine-year-old Jeremy faces his own pain and loss, his father's depression and sister's distance, the pity of friends and strangers, and his father's remarriage two years later, finding solace in fishing and his artwork. • ISBN-13: 978-1-4169-0770-1 • ISBN-10: 1-4169-0770-X • [1. Family problems—Fiction. 2. Drawing—Fiction. 3. Fishing—Fiction. 4. Depression, Mental—Fiction. 5. Divorce—Fiction. 6. Remarriage—Fiction.] I. Title. • PZ7.P94348Day 2007 • [Fic]—dc22 • 2005034362

FIRST EDITION

For my uncle Frank

The
Day
My
Mother
Left

"Farewell to an idea . . . The mother's face,
The purpose of the poem, fills the room."

—*Wallace Stevens*

1. *I was tired of waiting up. We had baseball* tryouts all afternoon, and my muscles ached from running around the field. I sat at my desk drawing a bird and almost fell asleep with the pencil in my hand. Then I heard the car pull up and the garage door close.

I switched off my desk lamp and got in bed under the cool sheets. The spring night was warm enough that I could leave my window open. Outside I heard the peeper frogs singing in the pond. It was raining, the type of rain that brought thunder. A wind blew a *whoosh* sound through the window screen.

The door slammed, and my mom and dad walked into the kitchen. Dad dropped his car keys and wallet in the top drawer by the fridge. Mom hung up her jacket in the hall closet. Before I fell asleep I hoped to tell her tryouts had gone well. As with every night, I would not let myself go to bed until she came into my room, kissed me on the cheek, and said, "Good night, sweet dreams, Jeremy—I love you." But tonight my dad was angry.

"Phoebe!" he yelled.

"Leave me alone, Carl."

"No, I won't leave you alone."

Mom's footsteps approached the stairs. Dad's followed, harder and louder. Then—*crash*.

"Oh my God," Mom screamed.

"I didn't mean to—it was an accident," my dad said.

"No," she said. "No, it wasn't."

"What did I do to deserve this?" my dad yelled. "How was I supposed to know you were unhappy?"

"You should have paid attention."

To what?

I folded my blankets down and stood at the edge of my bed. My chest felt hot and tight, and I held my breath. I tiptoed to the top of the stairs where I could see what had broken. The blue and white plate that hung in our hallway lay in pieces on the floor.

I closed my eyes and saw the empty spot where the plate had been, the wallpaper blotched with water stains. The plate reminded me of the polished inside of a shell. It had belonged to my mom's mom and had traveled from the apartment where my mom grew up in Prague, Czechoslovakia.

"So, maybe it wasn't an accident," my dad yelled. "Now there's nothing left to remind you of your miserable childhood." I saw his hand reach across the floor as he bent down to pick up a piece of the plate.

"What are you saying?" my mom screamed, crying. "That I didn't suffer?"

"No," he said. "I'm not saying anything. Nothing at all."

There was silence and the sound of the rain falling again. The fight seemed to be over. I took a deep breath, tiptoed back to my room, and got in bed. My head sunk deep in the pillow. My eyes burned from being tired. I couldn't stay awake.

Will things be okay if she doesn't kiss me good night?

The rain and the peeper frogs sang me to sleep.

Hours later, while it was still dark, I woke up to the sound of thunder.

Was it a dream?

What if it wasn't?

I got out of bed and shuffled down the stairs to the kitchen. On the way I passed the bare spot on the wall where the plate used to hang. Under the kitchen sink, on top of the garbage, lay the shards of blue and white porcelain. I picked out the pieces, collected them in my shirt, and carried them upstairs. I hid them in the bottom of my sock drawer.

The next morning, at sunup, I grabbed my lunch and my book bag and caught the school bus. My dad had left earlier than usual for work. Both my mom and my sister, Julie, were gone too.

The bus ride was quiet, and I was nervous. Not

first day of school nervous, or baseball tryouts nervous, or when I talked to a girl nervous. It was a different nervous, a kind I'd never felt. I was waiting for something to happen, but I didn't know what.

I looked for Josh in homeroom. My parents had been at his house the night before for a dinner party. Everything had been fine when they left for Josh's. Something must have happened there.

Josh sat at the desk next to me.

"You're wondering what happened, aren't you?" he asked.

"Yeah," I said. "Yes."

"Your mom was really loud and threw up on the table in the middle of dinner."

"On the table?" I asked, horrified. My stomach hurt, and I swallowed acid coming up from my throat.

"Yeah, it was pretty gross . . . I guess."

My mom threw up on the dinner table!

At first I felt better knowing. Adults got sick too, and sometimes they threw up. But then my mind played with the idea of my mom throwing up on the table in front of my friends' parents, acting loud and out of control, and I shuddered. Maybe she drank too much and made herself sick, like she did last New Year's. *Is that why Dad was so angry?*

I overheard students and teachers whispering about my mom in the halls, in the bathroom, in the classroom, by the lockers, in the gym, in the cafeteria at lunch.

Or was I imagining it?

During science class that afternoon, rain streaked down the windows, hammered against the pavement, *tink-tink*ed on the orange school buses lining up to take us home. It fell so hard, it drowned out the teacher's voice.

After school, instead of going home, I took the bus to my friend Stephen's house. We threw our book bags in the garage, grabbed his dad's BB gun, and crossed the road into the neighbors' hay field. The ground was soaked from the hard rainfall earlier that day, and water seeped in through my canvas sneakers. But now the sun was out, and the grass was green. I was happy for a moment that it was April.

Stephen took a shot at an old can on a cedar post and missed. He put the gun under his arm to grab a tin of lead pellets out of his pocket. I stood nearby and watched him reload. I was there, but I wasn't really there. Questions burned.

Maybe Stephen knows something.

"Did your mom go to Josh's parents' party last night?" I asked.

"You mean, *the* party?" Stephen laughed.

I hung my head and covered my face with my hands.

"Natalie wasn't there," he said. Stephen was the only kid I knew who called his mother by her first name.

"So . . ." I hesitated. "How did you hear about it?"

"I overheard Natalie talking to Mrs. Filson, who heard it from Mrs. Boyd, who was there."

"God," I said, dropping to the ground. My knees sunk to the wet grass. "*Everybody* knows."

"So what?" he said, pumping the air gun. "Your mom threw up at dinner."

"So what?" I asked, getting up. I grabbed a rock and threw it as far as I could.

"It's not the end of the world," Stephen said.

"What did you hear at school?"

"You know," he said, "the same thing everyone else heard."

I picked up another rock and threw it at the old can. I wiped the mud from my hands on my pants.

"Look, Jeremy," he said.

"What?"

"Nothing."

We walked across the field to the pond, where wood frogs were quacking like ducks. The sun was warm, and the birds sang.

"Take a shot," Stephen said, handing me the gun.

I grabbed the gun, raised the wooden barrel to my cheek, and aimed at a bird sitting on a faraway telephone wire.

We heard the *pop* of the air gun and saw a puff of

feathers against the blue sky. The bird dropped to the ground.

"Holy crap," Stephen said. "You hit it!"

"That's impossible," I said. "It's too far away."

We ran at full speed to the bird. It lay on the ground, a dark purple bruise on its breast.

"Lucky shot," Stephen said.

"Lucky?" I said. "I didn't mean to hit it. It was a mistake!"

I looked at the bird and thought I saw it moving, but it was just a breeze ruffling its soft feathers. I picked up the bird and cradled it in my hand. It was warm.

I wanted to keep it, maybe draw it, but the bird reminded me of all that had gone wrong. *I didn't mean to kill it.* I tossed it underhand into the brambles at the edge of the field and watched painfully as it got hung up in the thorns.

"Jesus."

I reached in to grab the bird, but the thorns caught my jacket, and I had to fight my way out with my free hand. I dug a shallow hole in the ground with my heel and covered the bird with leaves.

"Come on, Jeremy," Stephen said. "Let's see what Natalie made for dinner."

As we walked back to the house across the field, a dark cloud covered the sun and a torrential rain began to fall. We ran to the garage, soaking wet, and sheltered under the eaves where it was dry. My wet clothes stuck to my skin.

"Where did that cloud come from?" Stephen said with his back to the wall, water dripping off his hair and down his forehead into his eyes. We went inside through the open garage door. Stephen put down the BB gun without wiping the water off the barrel, and stopped to feed his pet rabbit.

"Who left Roger's cage open?" Stephen asked as the rain pounded on the roof. "Natalie must have cleaned it again. He could've escaped. If he did, we'd find him and—*pow*!" Stephen pretended to shoot his pet. "Dumb bunny," he laughed, holding out a piece of lettuce. "Your cage was open and you didn't even escape!"

I stood there watching. The rain made puddles outside the garage door.

"Do you think everyone at school knows?" I asked Stephen.

"Knows what?"

"You know. About my mom."

"Yeah, probably."

"What's the big deal, right?"

"I guess." Stephen shrugged.

The damp smell of sawdust in the rabbit's cage made me queasy.

"It's not that big a deal, is it?" I asked.

"No, not really."

"So why is it bothering me?"

Stephen was unusually quiet. He put down the lettuce and closed the cage door.

"Look, Jeremy," he said.

"What?"

"That's not the whole story."

"What do you mean?" I started to shiver.

"It's bigger than you think," he said.

"What are you talking about?"

"We'll find out who he is," Stephen continued. "We'll blow up his mailbox or something."

And as Stephen told me everything he'd heard about my mom, and something else he'd witnessed by the baseball field one day, it became perfectly clear why my dad was so angry.

I didn't need to go home, and I didn't really want to. I had my mitt and my spikes for tryouts the next day and my books for school. I borrowed a pair of dry clothes from Stephen, and Natalie hung mine to dry. That night I slept on a mattress in Stephen's room. I tossed and turned, unable to clear my head. What was going to happen? I was worried about my mom, but also about the second round of tryouts the next afternoon. I'd be competing for an outfield position with my least favorite person at school, Evan Sullivan.

I would say I hated him, but my dad told me never to use that word. I disliked him a lot.

It started two years before in third grade when my

mom gave me a jug bottle of wine to bring to school as a birthday gift for my teacher, Mrs. O'Connell. At recess, Evan stole my backpack and made me chase him around the swing set to get it back.

"What's in it?" he asked.

"None of your business."

"Feels heavy. Wonder if it'll break when I drop it."

"Don't you dare."

"Tell me what's in it and I won't."

"No," I said.

He swung it around his head like a lasso.

"Okay, okay!" I said. "It's a birthday present for Mrs. O'Connell."

"You geek," he said, and let go of my backpack, sending it high in the air. It went over the swing set bar, fell like a stone and hit the ground with a dull *thud*. A streak of brownish red liquid leaked through the canvas pack and down the pavement. A girl nearby screamed.

"Is that blood?" she yelled. "Oh my God, what's in there?"

Mrs. O'Connell heard the loud screams and came toward us.

I chased Evan, but he escaped into the gym.

"You sissy," I cried out.

"Jeremy, what's the matter?" asked Mrs. O'Connell.

"Evan broke it," I blurted out. "My mom's birthday gift for you."

Mrs. O'Connell examined the brownish liquid seeping out of my book bag and sniffed twice.

"Is that alcohol?" she asked.

I shrugged.

"Jeremy, that's very thoughtful," she said, patting me on the shoulder. "I'll never forget you brought me this gift. But please . . . tell your mother you can't bring wine to school."

The custodian emptied my backpack of broken glass and rinsed off my textbooks, but I never was able to really get the smell out.

Since that day, every time I saw Evan, I wanted to strangle him. I dreamed about sticking a pencil in his hand, or in his eye. But we didn't run across each other much anymore, except at tryouts.

The afternoon was raw and cloudy. The coach lined all the players up by the backstop on the field and gave us a batting order. We took turns at the plate hitting balls the coach fed into a pitching machine. I made contact a few times, but not very well, and when I did, the bat stung in my hands. Then we had field tryouts.

Evan and I both had good arms, so we were sent with some other kids to try out for center field. If I made starting position in center, Evan would make my life miserable. But I didn't get the position that day. I'd probably end up playing right field most of the season, or sitting on the bench, but that was okay if it meant I could avoid Evan.

In school there was no contest. I usually got As. My parents didn't have to tell me to do my work. Teachers liked me, and Evan was on their bad list. I don't remember ever meeting Evan's mom. My mom said she was fat, that she'd let herself go. Evan's dad came to all our games and watched from the bleachers.

My own dad didn't watch baseball. He didn't know the game and didn't want to. He was born in Brazil, where soccer was the religion. So instead my mother came to watch me play.

The few times I had the chance to bat, I could hear my mother's voice screaming, "Go, Jeremy! Smack the ball!" I wish I had turned to see where she was sitting, or who was sitting with her. I was just glad that she was always there.

Most of the time I struck out, and when I returned to the dugout, Evan would take a bat and swing it like he was smacking a home run and say, "Go, Jeremy! Smack the ball!" Sometimes our teammates laughed. I even caught the coach smiling once. But they could all go to hell. I knew that when my mom said that, she meant it, which was more than you could say for the other parents who just showed up at the end of the game to pick up their kids.

"Jeremy," my mom said on our drive home from the game, "You are the first person I loved. Your sister came first, but she didn't want my love. She popped right out. When you were born, you struggled to stay in. You taught me what love was."

People thought my mom was strange for speaking exactly how she felt, but it made me feel special. I wasn't embarrassed when she cheered for me, but it bothered me when Evan called me a mama's boy.

That Friday after school we had our first game of the new season. When I grabbed a bat and headed for the plate I heard Evan say, "Let's go, Jeremy—hit one for Mama." I turned. He made like he was sucking his thumb.

"I wouldn't talk that way to someone who has a bat in their hands," I threatened.

"The way you swing," he said, slapping his knee, "I'm not afraid."

"Boys!" the coach shouted. "Cut it out."

But when I got to the plate I didn't hear my mother

shouting. I held the bat, my back elbow high, my feet planted in the dirt. I turned around to see if she was there. When I did, the ball hit me square in the back, and I got to run to first base.

After the game I stood outside the chain-link fence. I was happy. My white pants were dusty in the right places, a sign of my success. I'd slid into second and scored a run. But my mom hadn't seen any of it.

I sat next to the snack bar, under the tall pine trees. My stomach was growling. A silver sports car pulled up and a man stepped out.

"Jeremy," the man said, "I'm Mr. Sullivan. Your mother asked me to give you a ride home."

My stomach turned. *Evan's dad?* Why was he giving me a ride home?

Evan's voice came from behind me. "Dad, what are you doing talking to that geek?"

"Be quiet, Evan," Mr. Sullivan said, taking a steady breath. "I don't have the patience for your loud mouth right now. We're giving Jeremy a ride home. Grab your mitt."

Evan sat in the front seat next to his father, and neither of us said anything. I wasn't sure how Mr. Sullivan knew how to get to my house, but I was glad to get out of the car when he pulled into my driveway.

"Thank you," I said.

"Mom! Mom!" I shouted, walking into the kitchen. "I scored a run!"

"She's not home yet," my dad said, sitting in his reading chair in the living room, a book in his hands. "Go clean up for dinner."

I got undressed and took a bath, which I still did sometimes, even though I knew most kids my age took showers. Then I put on my pajamas and sat down to do my homework at the kitchen table.

When Mom came home, my father walked into the kitchen. He was angry again.

"Where have you been?"

"At school," Mom said, twisting her blond hair and fixing it in a bun with a pencil.

"You're three hours late. Why didn't you call?"

"I had papers to correct."

I thought she'd stop at the table as she passed, run her warm hands through my hair, kiss my forehead. But she didn't. She opened the cabinet, took out a pot, and started filling it with water.

Dad left the kitchen.

"Mom," I said.

She stared out the window. The water started flowing over the top of the pot.

"Mom!" I yelled.

She continued to stare.

"Mom," I yelled louder, "I scored a run!"

She turned off the water.

"That's great, Jeremy," she said.

The white around her blue eyes was red and glazed. She poured some of the water off the top and put it on the stove. She lit the stove with a match. "Clear your stuff off the table, Jeremy. The pasta will be done in a few minutes."

I began to collect my notebook and pencils, my textbooks.

•   •   •

It was a cold night, but the peepers were loud in the pond.

Mom and Dad sat down at their usual places at the table. There was an empty seat across from me where my sister usually sat.

"Where's Julie?" my dad asked.

"Who?" my mother asked.

"Your daughter, Phoebe, remember?"

"You know, Carl," my mom said, looking out the window, "it's Friday. Where does she go every weekend? To Carey's house."

Mom put some salad on her plate. She ate one bite, then took her fork and started to comb her hair with it.

We stared.

"What are you doing, Phoebe?"

"Sorry," she said.

"What's wrong?" he demanded.

"Nothing."

"Okay," he said, clenching his hand around his napkin. "I'm just a poor teacher." He was about to lose his temper, but instead he reached his hand out to my mom's. She put her hands under the table.

My dad took a drink of water, and after a long silence he slammed his glass on the table. I turned my head, thinking the glass might shatter. I wanted badly to leave the kitchen.

"What's wrong?" my dad said again.

Mom stayed silent. I tried to pretend things were normal and finish my salad. My mom got up.

"I'm going for a walk," she said.

I looked at my dad, but he was staring at his plate. I cleared my place and went up to my room.

That Sunday in the early afternoon I stood beside my mom in the laundry room as she waited for the dryer to finish its cycle. She was impatient, waiting, waiting, tapping her foot on the checkered floor. She stopped the machine before it was finished, turning the dial until it buzzed. Then she took the clothes out, put them in a basket, and went upstairs. I followed her.

Usually I'd sit on the bed and talk with my mom as she folded the warm, clean clothes. But today the clothes were cold and damp, and my mom stood there like she'd been hypnotized, holding a soggy towel, transfixed by the clock on the dresser.

The next-door neighbors, the Langfords, were on vacation, and Julie was getting paid to take care of their dog, Candy. But Julie was still at Carey's, so Mom was doing her job for her.

"Jeremy," Mom said, "I think it's time I go let Candy out."

"Can I come?"

"No," she said. "Why don't you wait here."

"You sure?"

"Yes."

I hadn't done anything wrong. I just wanted to see Candy.

"But why?" I asked again. "Why can't I?"

"Because," she said, staring with her blue eyes, "I just want to take a walk."

I went to my room. I wanted to run after her—it

was a warm spring afternoon, daffodils blooming up and down the street, redwing blackbirds singing by the pond—but something in her voice told me not to. I sat and stared out the window. The lawn was covered with robins pulling worms out of the soil like rubber bands. I was watching them when I heard my father come in.

"Jeremy, where's your mother?"

"She's over at the Langfords'."

"Why didn't you go with her?"

"She told me to stay."

My father looked nervous, playing with the buttons on the sleeves of his shirt. He walked down the stairs to the kitchen and out the front door. The screen door slammed behind him.

I ran downstairs and saw him walk quickly toward the Langfords'. I went back to watching the robins on the lawn. Then I heard a car pull up in the driveway. It was Mrs. Olson dropping off Julie.

She looked at me oddly when I opened the door for her.

"Mom went over to take care of the dog."

"Why?" Julie asked, putting down her overnight bag. "I told her I'd be back in time to do it."

"I don't know," I said. "She's been there so long, Dad just left to look for her."

Julie flipped back her hair. "I'm sure she's fine." She walked into the kitchen and opened the fridge. "There's never any food here," she said.

Just then, Dad walked in. He walked right past Julie, sweat showing through the back of his plaid shirt.

"Get in here," he yelled on his way to the living room, a spring draft following him. "Your mother has something she wants to say."

Julie and I sat on the couch opposite my dad. The windows were open, and a strong breeze carried in the dirt-sweet smell of hyacinth flowers. We heard the front door open.

My mom walked into the living room and sat down in the only empty chair. Her face was wet with tears. Her lower jaw was shaking.

"So, Phoebe," my father said, "tell us. We're all waiting."

"I'm leaving," was all she said, sobbing deeply, her voice thin and fragile. "I'm leaving. I can't take this."

"Leaving where?" I asked.

"Who is it?" my father interrupted. "Phoebe, tell us."

"Who, who?" my mother said.

"Who did I overhear you on the phone with at the Langfords' house?" my dad said, raising his voice.

"Do you have to yell?" Julie asked.

"Don't talk to me like that, young lady," my father said, getting louder and louder like a breaking wave. "This is my house, and I can yell if I want to!"

"Are you guys getting . . . ?" Julie asked.

"Shut up, Julie," I said.

We all waited. My mother was silent for a long time. As we sat, the spring day became dark and cool.

"I met him at one of Jeremy's baseball games," she said, finally.

My dad put his head in his hands.

"Jesus, Phoebe," he said.

"He wasn't there at first," my mom said, almost smiling, but crying. "I didn't know how to handle all the attention."

"Who is he?" my dad demanded. "What's his name?"

"Why? What good will that do?" my mom said.

"Tell me," he threatened, raising his hand like he was capable of anything.

"Paul Sullivan," she said.

"Evan's dad?" I asked. My mom just stared at me. She didn't shake her head or nod or raise an eyebrow or move her mouth.

I ran to her and wrapped my arms around her neck.

"Don't!" I said, holding her, sobbing on her shoulder. I tried to look into her eyes, but she kept turning her head. She had a blank expression, like a doll.

My dad continued yelling.

"What did I do to deserve this?" he said, sitting

up straight in his chair. "I love you! I give you everything. What have I done wrong?"

"Nothing."

I looked into her blue eyes, and this time she held them still for a moment. I wanted to say, *I'll run away! I'll hurt myself!* but she turned again. Suddenly, I stopped crying.

I let go of my mother. I turned to Julie, who didn't look at all surprised. My mouth was dry and my face covered in dried salt.

I turned back toward my mom.

Leave.

I wanted to shout.

2. *That night the doorbell rang.*

I was lying in bed, but I snuck down the stairs far enough to see a strange woman walk into our kitchen. She had dark brown hair with curls in it, and she was heavy, the way my mom had once described her. I knew it had to be Evan's mother.

She looked around the kitchen nervously, at the yellow counter and the checkered floor. "Can I have a glass of water?" she asked.

My father sat her down at the kitchen table. My mother was already seated, her elbows on the table, her hands clasped in front of her. Dad brought Evan's mother a glass of water and sat down across the table from both of them.

"If you leave, Phoebe," the woman said, turning

her head toward my mom, "you won't just be hurting yourself. You will be hurting four children. If you don't, then maybe Paul will stay and we can work through this."

"No," my mother said.

The tightness returned to my chest as I listened.

"Isn't there something I can do, Phoebe?" my dad pleaded. "You never told me you were unhappy. It's a shock to me. You never told me. Where did I go wrong? What can I do?"

"It's too late, Carl."

"Is it because we have no money? I tried to please you but you never want anything."

My mom did not reply.

I ran down the last few stairs and into the kitchen in my pajamas. It was my last chance to fix things. I was confident I could. Usually, if I was persistent, I got what I wanted. I stood at the head of the table where they sat.

My mother stayed seated the same way she'd been before Evan's mom arrived.

"Mom, don't go," I said. "Please don't go!"

Evan's mother didn't look at me, nor did my dad. It was as if they were playing a game that took great concentration and I wasn't even there. Was I there? Was this happening? Nobody told me to stay or to go. It was so still, I noticed the buzz from the refrigerator, and the last of the spring peepers singing outside the window.

My mother cried but didn't say a word.

"Let's take a ride in my new car," Julie said to me the next day. She was sixteen and had just passed her driver's test.

Her car wasn't exactly new. She was driving my grandfather's old red Volkswagen beetle, which Uncle John had fixed up for her. It smelled like Grandpa and the apartment where he and Grandma had lived. I could hardly remember him now. Julie took the car up our street, struggling with the stick shift at the stop sign at the top of the road.

"I've got it under control," she said, then stalled

in the middle of the cross street, a car beeping at her. We laughed.

She drove down Buck Hill Road and around the twisting curves of South Park Avenue.

"Look out, Julie," I said, "there's a big bump up here."

"I know," she said, stepping on the gas.

"You're crazy!" I shouted as we flew over the bump.

She looked at me, smiling.

"Let's do it again," I said. So she turned the car around.

She really gunned it that time, and you could feel the back wheels pull off the pavement.

"I'd better slow down, huh?" she said, looking at me.

I shrugged my shoulders.

Julie pulled the car off the road by the bridge over the Mill River. I knew the sandy pull-off, where Stephen and I hid our bikes in summer while we were in the river catching crayfish. The river was swollen from spring rains and too cold for that now.

"Let's take a walk," Julie said. I followed her out of the car and down a path by the river. She stopped by a patch of ferns and skunk cabbage just coming up and sat on the bank overlooking the old, abandoned mill.

I threw stones in the currents.

"Jeremy," she said, "I'm going to tell you something." I crouched down, putting my hands in the sandy soil, as the stream crashed by in front of us, getting louder and louder. "Mom and Dad are getting divorced."

In the swampy lot on the other side of the river, wood frogs started up, loud like a giant flock of quacking ducks, drowning out the noise in my head. A bush on the opposite bank was blooming with pink flowers and I felt like I was floating in the warm spring air. For the first time since that night when the plate shattered, I felt calm.

"Come on, Jeremy." Julie put her arm around me. "We're going to be fine."

I watched the river's currents.

• • •

The next afternoon, my mother left the house with a single bag. In the days before, I'd imagined myself grabbing her legs and begging her not to go, but now as she stood there on the driveway, I just blinked. I was right in front of her when she got in her car, my feet on the driveway, and I didn't wave good-bye.

3. *Back at school,*
that easy feeling I had by the river
was gone. I feared that Evan might know
the whole story. We passed each other in the
hallway but never made eye contact.

A week after school ended, so did the Little League
season. Then summer baseball began, and along with
it came different teams and coaches. My father drove
me to practice. This year they were dividing the players into major- and minor-league teams. I hoped to
make the majors but worried I would have to compete
with Evan for an outfield position. I didn't see him
anywhere.

I asked Josh and Stephen, but they didn't know
where he was. Finally, I asked the coach. He said Evan

wasn't allowed to play because of his detentions and bad behavior at school. He had to go to summer school.

Without my mother around, the house felt empty. I was alone with my father. Now that Julie had a car, she wasn't around, and my father had no energy to tell her what to do. She could come and go as she pleased. Mostly she was gone.

Without Mom there to cook, my dad made very simple meals. Monday was rice and chicken, Tuesday was rice and beans, Wednesday was hot dogs with baked beans and rice, and Thursday we went out to a fast-food restaurant, which was a great treat. The rest of the week our menu repeated itself.

"I'm going to kill her, Jeremy," Dad said over dinner, his head hanging low. I felt my face fill up with redness again. I saw the bird I'd shot, tumbling to the ground. "Why did she leave me? Why did she leave me? He's a lawyer, he has a sportscar, he takes her out to dinner. I'm just a poor teacher. Why Jeremy, why?"

"I don't know, Dad," I said. I did not know what to say. I picked up my fork, because it felt like what I should be doing. But I wasn't interested in eating. I was just going through the motions. It was like my life was a car and someone else was driving it.

"The only reason she's alive is because of you and Julie," my dad continued. He looked at my full plate of food and then at me. I put down my fork and started to get up from the table, but my father stopped me, taking my arm. I sat down again.

"Jeremy, my boy," he said, "I'm sorry. I'm so sorry. Please eat. You know I don't mean it," he said. "But God, for what she's done, I think I could."

He slammed his fist on the table, but I saw he was trying hard not to be angry. His glass of water spilled on the blue tablecloth, and a darker blue spot spread, running over the edge of the table, dripping on the floor.

"Goddamn it!" he yelled, and ran his hardened fingers through his hair.

"Dad, come on, it's just water."

"How could I be so stupid?" he said.

"You're not, Dad! Stop it!"

He started to laugh.

"God almighty!" he said. "Why? Why?"

He looked across the table and the wet blue tablecloth and was silent for a while. I noticed his accent now more than I ever had, maybe because I was alone with him, maybe because he seemed foreign.

"You know," he said, "when I used to sail on cargo ships, we'd wet the tablecloths in the dining mess when there was a storm, to keep the plates and silverware from sliding off the table. Maybe I should have stayed in the Merchant Marine. I'd be a captain now, making lots of money. But then I wouldn't have had you and Julie."

"We've got to make the most of it," I managed to say, but the words felt weird as they came out of my mouth. *That's something someone else would say.*

"Ah, Jeremy," my dad said, shaking his head, still looking at the tablecloth. "How lucky I am to have you in this storm."

• • •

It went like that for days. Some days were calm, and then something would remind us of her and the seas would kick up, the tall, mad waves rocking our ship. My dad began to talk more about the past, about his father and my family history.

"I look back on it now," my dad said, "and I was lucky to have the father that I did. He didn't go to college, but he was no dummy. He was Czech, like your mother. He taught English to your Uncle John and me while we were still kids in Brazil. He must have been thinking of moving to America for years. And I think, 'What kind of man would have the energy at fifty years old, older than me, to move his whole family to another country to find a new home?' Listen to what I'm telling you Jeremy, so you can tell your kids one day. He spoke seven languages fluently. His favorite saying was in Spanish '*No hay mal que por bien no venga*,' which means 'There's no bad that doesn't come for some good.' How true," he said. "We're going to look back one day and see the truth in it all."

Instead of listening to himself, though, and looking for the good he spoke about, my dad let his attitude get worse. He made the sadness part of his daily routine.

Usually by May his garden was tilled and planted. But this year the old tomato vines from last summer's garden were still standing, brown and drooping, tied to stakes, like tired scarecrows someone forgot to take down after Halloween. Weeds had grown up around them, hiding the raised beds where neat rows of peas and lettuce should have been growing. By now his skin should have been dark from being outside in the sun. But he looked as pale as I'd ever seen him, almost green. The clothes he wore when he worked outside lay folded in the basement on his workbench, still holding the smell of sawdust from cutting and splitting wood in the fall.

Occasionally, though, he'd snap out of his depression and tell me stories of his days sailing around the world on cargo ships. The stories were filled with faraway peoples and exotic places and animals, of shipments of hardwoods from the jungles of Africa and

Indonesia, cashews and pistachios from Turkey, and tea from Pakistan.

"We ate so many pistachios," he said, laughing, "that our hands were red. I love the sea. Sometimes I wonder how I ever gave up sailing. But when I met your mother, things changed. I tried to keep sailing. I wanted to become a captain. Then I stopped sailing and worked as a port captain, supervising the unloading of the ship, so I could be with her. Your mother and I were living in Miami, and then in New York City. Wherever the work was." He sighed.

Before my mom left, my dad made trips to the town library every few days to bring back the books he had read and check out new ones. I'd go with him and look at the books with pictures of fish and birds. But it had been weeks since we'd gone, and the glass table where he usually kept a small stack of books was clean and empty, except for a few overdue titles.

"Let's go to the library," I said to my dad one day.

"We should, I know," he said. "I just don't feel like reading."

I brought him a glass of cold iced tea, and when I returned an hour later, the ice was melted and the glass was still full.

"Tell me the story of tiger hunting in Bengal," I said, sitting down on the couch near him.

"It's not so interesting," he said.

"Well tell me about the big shark you caught in Brazil."

"I can't, Jeremy, not now."

One morning, I saw him walk off into the backyard, past the overgrown garden, into the thick cedars and saplings that grew in the abandoned field. When he came back in, his face was red, and I thought he'd been crying.

Another time, I followed him and saw him on his knees underneath an apple tree. He was crouched down, his head touching the ground as if he was praying. There was a cedar log cut in half there that he'd made into a bench. I remember seeing photos of my mother sitting on it. I wanted to comfort him, but something held me back. And then I couldn't take my eyes off him. I wanted to touch him to make sure he was still in that body, so I decided to sneak up behind him, quietly, like an Indian. I put my hands on his shoulders, near either side of his neck.

"Jeremy," he said, surprised. He was crying.

"It's okay, Dad. Please don't cry."

"Sometimes I think it would have been better if she had died," he said, not to me or anyone in particular. "But knowing she's alive out there, that she's living a new life with another man, is killing me."

It was June, and the daffodils I'd helped my mom plant last fall were flowering. We'd used a special green tool to make holes in the ground for the bulbs. *Was she planning to stay to see them flower?* Songs she used to sing came into my head. I could hear her voice singing as if she were in the room with me. Mail arrived addressed to Phoebe Vrabec. The woman who checked the electric meter, the man who filled the oil tanks, the garbage man, people who took walks up and down our dead-end street—they asked about her.

When they came by, I didn't know what to tell them. I tried to push the memory of her away, but it kept coming back like a persistent mosquito.

An elderly woman rang our doorbell one day. My dad was out, so I answered the door.

"Is Phoebe home?" she asked.

"No," I said.

"Will she be back soon?"

"She's gone."

The woman laughed. "Did your father tell you to say that?"

"No," I said. I was tired of trying to explain.

She looked at my face and saw I wasn't kidding.

"Oh, I'm so sorry," she said. "I'm so, so sorry. Was there an accident?"

"No," I said. "She left."

"She's left? Well, do you know where she is?"

"No, she left *us*."

Go away.

"Oh, my dear. Your mother is such a sweet woman. I don't really believe she's gone. How could she leave?"

I stared without answering.

"My dear child," she continued, the wrinkles of her face arranging into a look of sympathy. "You must be going through such a difficult time."

I was still holding the door half open. I'd heard the phrases of pity so many times, first- and secondhand, that I'd become very good at showing no emotion.

She reached into her stuffed bag and pulled out a Bible. Her hands were shaking, thin and almost transparent with bluish green lines like dried seaweed.

Who is this woman?

"Isaiah 49:15," she began reading from the Bible. "'Can a mother forget the baby at her breast and have no compassion on the child she has borne?'" She paused to look at me. "Yes," she almost shouted. "But 'though she may forget, I will not forget you!'" She held up a finger. Her empty brown eyes stared. She was not a tall woman; she wasn't much taller than I was.

"Do you know who is speaking in that passage?" she asked.

"No," I said.

"God is. God will never forget you. No matter what your parents do here on Earth. God is your father, first and foremost. You are never alone. He will take care of you."

"Why are you here?"

"Your mother was studying the Bible with us," she said. "God bless her, wherever she is. Pray for her. I will pray for you both."

The woman turned and walked to her car. The engine was still running.

My father taught summer school two days a week, an outdoor class called Marine and Field Biology. He drove the bus full of summer-school students to different places: woods and wetlands, marsh and seaside. I went along and learned a lot from him about the trees and birds. He was fun and excited around all of us. When he was home, though, he sat in a chair in the living room, staring out the window, an open book in his lap.

Erratum

Due to a printing error,
the wrong date appears on the
copyright page of this book.

The correct publication year of
The Day My Mother Left is 2007.

The grass in our yard had grown too tall for the mower to cut. The patio furniture, usually dusted off and outside, was still in the basement. Dishes were piled up in the sink, something my father had never tolerated before. I had looked forward to summer so much, and now I wished I could go back to school. Stephen was away at summer camp for two weeks, and everyone else I knew belonged to a country club with swim teams and tennis lessons.

I sat down at the kitchen table with some pencils and drew. I took out one of my dad's bird books and copied a sparrow hawk. This time the drawing surprised me. The hawk stared at me and gave me a chill. I left it on the kitchen counter for my dad to see.

I remembered that before my mom told us she was leaving, I'd been working on a bunch of drawings. They were mostly drawings of warblers, small and colorful birds that reminded my dad of ones he knew growing up in Brazil. I had sewn the drawings between cardboard covers like a book, and on the cover I had written in black marker: *Book of Birds*.

It was in my desk drawer. I'd forgotten all about it. I ran upstairs to get it so I could compare the old drawings with my new ones.

But the *Book of Birds* was gone.

It was the kind of thing I'd never lose or misplace. Months of work had gone into making it. I knew exactly where I kept it, and I knew that there was no other explanation. My mother had taken it with her.

She stole it.

I ran downstairs into the living room.

"Dad!" I shouted.

"What, Jeremy?" he said, turning from the window to look at me.

"Have you seen . . . this bunch of drawings I made of birds?"

"What?"

"Never mind," I said, burning with frustration. Of course he didn't know anything about it; the only person I'd shown it to was my mom. I ran the possibilities through my head over and over. I even remembered seeing the drawer of my desk slightly open on the day my mother left. I'd shut it without looking.

Now the *Book of Birds* was gone, along with the songs and the flowers and my mom's smile. She left us and our house, and she took almost nothing with her, yet she took everything . . . except me.

I decided to replace the old *Book of Birds* with a new and better one. I drew and painted every day. This summer wasn't about waiting for my mom to take me to the town pool with all the laughter and sun, diving and splashing, smells of suntan lotion and chlorine. As I drew in the kitchen, my dad paced back and forth across the living room like he still expected her to walk through the door.

I took long walks to get out of the house.

One day, on one of those walks, I stopped to listen to the bullfrogs making their *ooouuummm ooouuummm* sounds in the pond. Behind the barn, two cows were doing the reverse: *Mmmuuuooo*. Every sound had its own place, and for the first time in a while, I felt I had a place too.

I walked on.

Past the old dairy barn and a big patch of milk-weed at the end of our dead-end street, I came to the path that led to the woods and the reservoir. A big sugar maple stood like a guard at the edge of the for-est, its trunk posted with a yellow sign with black let-ters that said: NO TRESPASSING.

I remembered my dad telling me that about a hundred years ago, the water company bought all this land from the people who lived in the Mill River Valley. They tore down the homes and burned the wreckage, and they built a dam that flooded the river to make a reservoir for drinking water. The land around the reservoir, once open farms and fields, slowly became forest. The old dirt road led from our dead-end street into those woods.

I walked beyond the end of the street, down the dirt road, under the shade of the trees, through tall ferns and stands of spicebush and witch hazel. I'd only been down to the reservoir a few times before, with my dad. I'd always wanted to go down and fish the reservoir alone, but I was too afraid. Kids in town told stories about the ghosts of the people who were forced out by the water company, whose houses were torn down when the valley was flooded.

Bird songs echoed under the trees. *A wood thrush.* I came to a place I remembered, where a row of old trees grew along the road. My father had told me the trees—big sugar maples—were planted many years before to mark the front of somebody's property. Nearby he showed me the foundation of an old farmhouse, a pit in the ground lined with stones. It looked like pictures of old ruins I'd seen in school textbooks.

I stood in that place, by the row of trees, alone now. I felt alive, my vision seemed sharper. I could imagine a house behind the row of trees, a breeze blowing through the windows, billowing the curtains. The place had seemed spooky to me when I was with my dad. Now I walked on without fear.

Soon I was in a place I didn't recognize, where the dirt road split on the other side of two stone pillars.

One road went down to the reservoir. The other went up a hill. I took the higher road.

Farther along I got lost in my footsteps. I was hypnotized, watching my feet fall on the path, until a bird flew so close to my face that I flinched. I looked up and there in front of me was a massive tree with giant limbs, its long roots growing around a mossy ledge like the legs of an octopus.

A few paces from the tree, partly hidden by the leaves, I saw a staircase made of large, flat fieldstones. I walked up the stone stairs and straight ahead, under the massive limbs of the old tree. Light spilled through the leaves onto the ground, where I began to see the outline of a perfectly square pit lined with stone—the cellar of an old house or maybe a barn. A staircase led down into the foundation, and in the center of the square was a huge pile of stones and bricks. *This is where the chimney was.* I stood there as a cold breeze off the reservoir lifted the hairs on the back of my neck.

And then I heard the sound of moving water.

I couldn't see any water, but the sound was so close that I felt like I was surrounded by it, even standing in it. I walked along the edge of the house foundation and down a hill behind it, in the direction of the sound of the water. I got down on my knees and pushed aside some dead leaves with my hand.

The brook was running underneath me.

Fieldstones, longer than I was tall, made a bridge over the brook. Leaves had piled up on top of the stone bridge, hiding the brook completely from view. I tried to imagine the farmers moving the big stones into place. It would have taken several men, maybe with horses, to move one of those stones.

As I walked farther down, the brook opened up and flowed freely through the woods. Tall green ferns and skunk cabbage grew on the bank. I came to a small waterfall. Deep in the dark pool below it, I saw a flash.

A fish.

If Stephen had been with me, he would have moved on by now, gotten impatient, gone downstream, jumped in the water, and disturbed the mud and gravel at the bottom of the brook. He could never stand in one place for more than a minute. But something about the place held my attention, asked me to be still and silent. I didn't want to go home. I wanted to stay. I pictured a desk, my lamp, a chair, a bed—*my own place*—arranged on the leaves that carpeted the floor. I wanted to stay here longer, but I needed supplies.

I ran most of the way home and arrived sweaty and out of breath. I worked quickly. I feared that if I saw my father or spent too much time in the house, my vision of the camp would disappear.

Stick to the task.

I stuffed some matches, crackers, an apple, raisins, candy bars, a penknife, a flashlight, an extra T-shirt, and a bottle of water in my backpack. I tied my sleeping bag to the backpack with rope and threw in a drawing pad, pencils, and a hook with some line.

I ran down the stairs toward the living room. My dad wasn't in his reading chair.

I should leave a note.
No.

I put my arms through the straps of my backpack and started back down my street, past the barn and through the woods again. I liked the feeling of weight on my back as I ran.

I took a different route, directly through the woods instead of on the dirt road, in case a warden from the water company was on patrol. I'd heard that sometimes the wardens went out looking for trespassers, but I'd never seen one. I didn't want anyone seeing where I was going anyway. The spot was like a photograph in my mind as I walked. I could reconstruct it perfectly. It didn't surprise me when I suddenly found myself there.

My camp.

I put down my backpack near the stone stairs and found a large flat rock that made a good bench to sit on. I untied my sleeping bag from the pack, took a breath of the cool air coming off the brook, and lay down on the flat rock, looking up into the tree branches. The air carried the smell of the spicebush and the rusty smell of water.

I ate my apple, core and seeds and all. I grabbed a hook and some line and headed to the reservoir, past a yellow sign posted on a white pine tree: NO TRES-PASSING it read in bold black letters. The sign seemed funny because nobody was watching me except for the birds, whose singing seemed louder and louder.

The water of the reservoir came right up to the trunks of the hemlock and pine trees. Small waves lapped against the stones. The air was warmer here, and the pine needles were soft under my feet. I leaned over and saw my broken reflection in the water. I recognized, for the first time, the ghostly image of my mother looking back at me.

Can't I go anywhere without thinking of her?

A small fish broke the surface of the water, disturbing the reflection. Underneath the glare from the sky, I saw more fish. *Sunfish.*

I reached into my backpack for my pencils and

paper. I tried to draw the small sunfish. An inchworm fell from a tree above me onto the surface of the water, and immediately one of the fish came to the surface and sucked it into its small mouth. Another inchworm was hanging from its silk thread just above the water, but it was too far for the fish to grab. One eager fish tried, jumping out of the water, flashing its golden sides and orange belly. I put down my pencils and paper. I wanted to catch one.

I caught my first fish with Julie when I was five. It wasn't my dad or my uncle who took me fishing the first time. It was my sister. Funny. I knew sunfish were eager biters. I looked behind me on the bank and saw an anthill. The ants were carrying small white grubs from the top of what looked like a volcano. I didn't know what the grubs were, but they were big enough to put on a hook. I tried one as bait.

Because it didn't weigh much, I couldn't get the grub out far enough to reach a fish. So I got a stick and tied my line to the end of it. With the stick I could get the line out to where the fish were. As soon as the grub touched the water, I had a sunfish on the hook.

The fish had blue streaks that ran across its olive cheeks like streams on a map. Its eyes were orange-brown, with halos of green and blue. Its sides were rust-colored with dark bands, and its belly was pumpkin orange. I took out the hook and held the fish in my hand for a while.

Maybe I'll keep it. Draw it.

My hand dropped in the water and the fish splashed as it swam out.

I leaned back against a rock. I took a deep breath and as I exhaled I noticed that the birds had stopped singing. I put down my makeshift fishing rod and sat completely still.

A large bird swooped down from the hemlocks. It landed on a rock right next to me. It was an owl and had tufts of feathers on each side of its head that looked like ears. It seemed so much like a person that I thought it might speak to me. I assumed it would just stay there, but as soon as it landed, it lifted its furry feet off the rock and flew away.

In the first weeks after my mom left, I felt that I wouldn't mind just going to sleep and not waking up. My head was so full of bad thoughts that sleep was the only way out. If I could sleep. I didn't want to draw, or do homework, or move. But now I had trouble remembering those times. I felt different, stronger, and my head was full of things I wanted to do.

What had I been so worried about?

I felt at home in the woods. It was the *only* place where I felt at home. Time didn't mean anything here, nor did money or lack of money, or Evan, or baseball, or school, or cars, or parents, or plates or anything. I was alone and nothing could get at me. I wanted to shout, *Nothing matters!*

I walked to the old foundation, which was built into a hillside. *If I cover the top with logs, I can make a good shelter over my head.* I set to work choosing long, straight, dead timber, dry and newly fallen, from the forest floor. I lined up the logs to make a roof. I found an old iron bucket, filled it with water, and brought it to my site. I gathered dry grass and made a floor. This was basic stuff I had learned on camping trips as a Cub Scout.

When I finished my shelter, I took out a candy bar and walked down to the reservoir to eat it. I watched the sun slip down behind the trees like a piece of melting ice. I was amazed at the idea of watching the sun move. I thought of my father. His voice in my head. "It's not the sun moving that you're witnessing," he'd say. "It's the earth turning."

When are things ever what they seem to be?

I threw a stick and laughed out loud.

Across the reservoir I heard ducks laughing in a cove.

Whack, hack, ack, ack.

I went back to my camp with a skip in my step, pleased with my shelter. And when I got under the roof, I felt tired. I unrolled my sleeping bag and climbed inside. It was too hot, so I unzipped the sleeping bag and lay on top.

I dreamed of flying.

I was walking down the slope of our front lawn, spreading my arms. *Why haven't I done this before?* It was so easy. The breeze lifted my body, and I was floating effortlessly above the tree line. I saw the whole farm below, the pond and the lily pads, the big green fields, the old barn. I flew over the reservoir and saw where the old stone walls came into the water.

Light as a feather.

But then, suddenly, I was heavy. I lost my confidence, and the more I did, the faster I fell. I steered away from the trees and fell into the blue water of the reservoir.

I woke up, startled.

I heard a whistle. I knew that whistle.

I knew that whistle! Two high, bent notes with a straight one in the middle.

Whew—whe, whew.

My father and Uncle John had made up that whistle when they were kids in Brazil. They used it to find each other in their neighborhood games, their secret whistle that only they knew.

Whew—whe, whew.

For as long as I could remember, that had been our family whistle. My dad taught it to us, and we used it to find each other in the supermarket, in the yard, in a crowd, in the house. It was ours and no one else's. There was no mistaking it. It was my dad. He was looking for me.

My father could whistle very loud. He whistled with two fingers in his mouth. The whistle carried a mile. It sounded close, but far at the same time. I heard the sound distinctly, maybe half a dozen times. Then the whistles became more distant and disappeared.

I didn't answer.

I couldn't sleep the rest of the night. I even tried to count the stars. By the time the sun came up I was exhausted. My eyes were burning, and my head felt hot and sore, like someone had been using it as a drum. I wanted my bed: the soft sheets, my pillow, my dresser, my closet, my window. I packed up my sleeping bag and started walking back.

Before I left camp, I took the food I had left and buried it under some rocks near my shelter. I knew some animal would probably dig it up and eat it, but maybe if I came back and needed it, it would be there.

When I get home, I'll draw a map. I'll start a journal like my dad used to keep. Inside the front cover, in a secret compartment, I'll store my map. Even if someone found the map and followed it to my place in the woods, they could never really get there, because the real place wasn't on any map, or in the woods. It was nothing you could see. It was inside me.

My father saw me walking up the driveway and ran out to hug me.

"Jeremy!" he said. "I was so worried about you!"

"You were?"

He took me in his arms and squeezed me.

"I knew you'd be fine," he said. "But I was scared. I was up all night thinking. 'God, I've failed. Have I failed at this, too?'"

I shook my head.

Dad looked at me and messed up my hair. Big tears sprang from his eyes. I felt like I'd been away a long time. His voice was foreign. Our house, the greenish clapboards, the hedges below the window, looked small.

"I still think of you as a boy," he said. "That's my mistake. You're growing up. Look at you!"

"I heard you whistling," I said, slowly remembering his voice.

"I just wanted you to know I was there if you needed me. I will be here for you, Jeremy. Always. Do you understand?"

"Yeah, I do, Dad," I said, scratching the back of my head. "I think I'm going to go to bed."

I went inside and upstairs to my room. I dropped my book bag on my desk and got under the sheets. The clean sheets smelled of summer, dried on the clothesline, cool and soft. I much preferred this to the ground. Home had never felt so good as it did then.

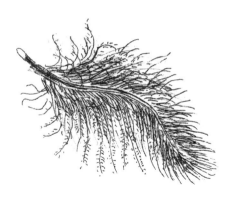

4. On my tenth birthday Uncle John took me fishing.

Uncle John was a good foot taller than my dad, with big shoulders, dark skin, and dark-brown eyes. Dad said he was born in the wrong century, that he should have been a mountain man on the frontier instead of a gym teacher and a football coach.

Mom told me that Uncle John had wanted a boy. He had three girls instead. He was jealous of my dad, Mom said, because of me.

Early that morning my dad drove me to Uncle John's house in the nearby town of Monroe. It was before sunrise, and my dad and Uncle John drank coffee in the dimly lit kitchen. I hadn't seen my uncle since my mom left.

"So, Jeremy," my uncle said after Dad left. "You want some coffee?"

"Thanks, but . . ."

"Right—you don't drink coffee. How about juice?"

Watching my uncle pour juice seemed wrong. His hands were so big that the half-gallon container disappeared in his grip. He was legendary for fixing things. My father said he had "mechanical genius." I had trouble even putting the chain back on my bike, so I was eager to watch and learn.

My cousins were asleep upstairs, and I was glad. They usually made fun of me or tried to teach me how to dress cool.

"Should we go?" Uncle John asked, looking at my empty juice glass.

"Sure," I said.

It was a cool morning. We drove in Uncle John's black truck, which towed the boat.

"What have you been up to?" Uncle John asked.

"Baseball just ended, so not much." I hesitated. I

didn't want to tell my uncle I was drawing pictures of birds, because I thought he'd think it was a sissy thing to do. I had a feeling he thought my father was a sissy, because he'd rather sit inside and read books than fix cars. I was glad my father hadn't come along. They always ended up fighting out on the boat.

"You ever think of trying out for junior football?"

Uncle John knew I played soccer in the fall. He was younger than my father by two years, and the soccer bug had not bitten him as a kid in Brazil. His sport was football—American football.

"Yeah," I said. "You think I should?"

Not much else was said until we got to the river.

Launching the boat was always an ordeal. I could never figure out how to help Uncle John when he asked.

"Jeremy," he yelled out, "disconnect the clip from the cleat. No, no. First you have to take the clicker off the winch and unwind it to get some slack."

He may as well have been speaking Swahili. I tried to do what he told me, slipping on the seaweed, bruising my arm on the trailer, shaking with fear that I wouldn't be able to figure it out. Uncle John had to climb up to the bow and disconnect the boat from the trailer himself.

Like this, Jeremy, I wished he'd said, but he just did it in silence, with a cigarette in his mouth.

"Why don't you get the rods out of the back of the pickup?" he said instead, stamping his cigarette out in the wet gravel. That was a seemingly simple task, but still kind of difficult for me. I couldn't figure out how to open the gate at the back of the truck, so I had to climb up onto the truck bed to grab the rods and then climb down while holding all the heavy equipment.

At last the boat was in the water. Uncle John kept a cigarette lit in his mouth while operating the boat at a high speed. We motored off down the river until he spotted a flock of terns and seagulls hovering close to the water. Uncle John turned off the engine.

"Look over the side of the boat, Jeremy," he said, looking himself. "They're so thick you could walk on them."

Below us I saw a giant school of fish swimming in a tight formation. Uncle John called them bunker.

"Underneath the bunker are larger fish—bluefish," he explained. "The bluefish chase the school of bunker to the surface, where they swallow them whole or chop them in half with their teeth. If we get one in the boat, be very careful. Their teeth are razor sharp."

The gulls and terns were gathering over the school, speaking to each other: *kee-arr kee-arr, kee-ow kee-ow*, then *gaw-gaw-gaw*. Just then the big school of fish exploded on the surface, fish jumping in all directions.

"See, the big blues are pushing them up, and the birds are here for the scraps. See the oil slick on the water?" Uncle John asked, looking at me. "Bunker are an oily fish. You smell it?"

It smelled like watermelon.

Uncle John grabbed a rod. I had never seen him so excited about something. With his big square hands he tied a weighted three-pronged hook to the end of the line. He cast the treble hook a long way, then jerked it through the water until he snagged a fish. He hauled one bunker after another into the boat, each about a foot long, caught in the side by the big three-pronged hook, and bleeding. He threw them into the cooler, where they made a pattering, drumming sound against the inside. When we had about a dozen bunker, we motored to Uncle John's favorite fishing spot: upriver, under the power lines, below the I-95 bridge.

Uncle John dropped the anchor and held the line until it caught. The sun had barely risen, but the warmth was reaching us. He took a deep breath and looked around, alert, sniffing the air like a deer. He knelt down next to the cooler and, taking a bunker in one hand and a knife in the other, cut the fish into three pieces. He baited three separate hooks on separate rods and cast them out into the channel before putting them in the rod holders. Then he wiped his hands with a small white towel.

I tucked in the back of my shirt to keep the breeze from creeping up. The deck of the boat was wet with dew, and now my butt was too. It was cold and noisy under the tall interstate bridge. All the sounds seemed to be coming from somewhere else. Large trucks rumbled by over us; pigeons cooed in the high steel beams. A large heron sitting on a cement piling made a *gwak-gwak* sound as it spread its wings and flew away. Even our voices echoed from somewhere else when we spoke, but we didn't speak much. My uncle, his eyes focused on the lines, lit one cigarette after another, putting the butts out between his fingers and dropping them in a bucket. I didn't think he remembered I was there, until I saw his brown eyes gleaming at me, glowing in the morning sun. He must have seen that I was cold, because he took off his wool shirt, came over to me, and wrapped it around me like a blanket. It was red plaid and smelled like car grease and wood smoke.

"Feels like September," he said, lighting a cigarette and looking across the fishing lines, "but I'm glad it's not." He took a long pull from his cigarette, the orange embers flickering. "You and me both, right? That means we'd be back in school."

I nodded, smiling at my uncle, and took a deep breath.

"You been drawing lately?"

"Yeah," I said. It was the last thing I expected him to ask me.

"Your grandfather had some drawing talent," he said. "Maybe that's where you get it."

Just then the drag on one of the reels started screaming—a bluefish had taken one of the chunks of bunker and was pulling line. Uncle John grabbed the rod out of the holder and set the hook by pulling back hard.

"It's a big blue, Jeremy. Why don't you bring it in?"

"No, you do it," I said. I was afraid I wouldn't be able to land it.

The big fish jumped, its whole body coming out of the water, the rising sun glinting gold on its sides. When it hit the water again, the sound of the splash echoed under the bridge.

"Grab the gaff!" my uncle said, bringing the big bluefish along the side of the boat. I was glad I finally knew what something was, and I picked up the stick with the big hook at the end we used for landing fish. I handed it to him, and he sunk the gaff hook into the fish's head, right behind the eye, pulling it aboard.

"There's dinner," he said, the fish flopping, blood spattering from its wound on the white deck.

"How big is it?" I asked.

"A good fifteen pounds."

He threw it in the cooler, which he called the kill box.

"You're good luck, Jeremy," he said to me, and smiled.

I smiled back.

Once we started catching fish, I felt more at ease. Uncle John hooked two more bluefish and landed one, and when the schools of bunker and blues went out with the tide, we ate salami sandwiches. He sat on the cooler, and I sat on the bow facing him.

"That was fun," I said, opening a can of Coke.

He nodded, then closed his eyes, taking another bite and chewing with his eyes closed.

"You know, Jeremy," he said, putting down his sandwich and taking a soda out of the cooler. His eyes were open now. "I feel sort of responsible for what happened."

"Yeah," I said. "I do too." I thought about the bird I shot falling off the wire. I thought that maybe if I hadn't shot the bird, none of this would have happened.

"You shouldn't, boy. Don't ever say or think that." He swatted a yellow jacket from the mouth of his Coke can. "I'm the one who introduced them, your mom and dad." He paused, looking up to the sky. "Jesus," he said, shaking his head. "Twenty years. I can't believe it's been that long."

In the early afternoon, back at the dock, I watched him clean our fish as the flies buzzed around his hands, which were stained with blood.

Later that afternoon at my uncle's house, I swam in the pool with my little cousin Jill. We could smell the fish and hamburgers cooking, and when dinner was ready we got out of the pool and sat under the grape arbor, wrapped in towels. My dad had arrived, and we ate bluefish and hamburgers on the porch and drank iced tea. The sun was still warm and glowing orange above the trees. When we finished dinner, Aunt Janice cleared the table and brought out a cake with ten candles flickering. Everyone sang "Happy Birthday," and I made a wish as I blew out the candles.

I wished my wish, but I didn't tell anyone. I knew that if you say a wish out loud it doesn't come true.

5. My dad tried every day to reason out what had happened to him. As a science teacher he felt everything had a cause and effect.

"The family is a scientific unit," my dad said. "It stays together for protection from the unknown. The mother nurtures the offspring; the father protects the family."

But the laws of nature did not apply in this case.

"Why did she leave me, Jeremy?" he asked over dinner. "Does he give her things I didn't? I'm just a poor teacher—I gave her all I could."

During the day, he played the father, telling me what to do and how to do it, and to keep my chin up if I was feeling low. When I asked him a question, he had an answer. But at night, in the house again, the roles reversed. Dinner without my mom continued to be strange. My dad asked me questions I had no answers for. Julie had her car, so she was never home. But even if she'd been home, she wouldn't have had any answers either.

My dad didn't sleep. His reading lamp was on almost all night, and he looked tired and thin.

A few times he even woke me. "I just wanted to make sure you were okay." I think he was afraid to lose me, too.

One night he was standing over my bed, whispering my name.

"Jeremy . . . Jeremy. Did you hear something?"

"No, Dad. I was sleeping."

"I thought I heard someone walking on the roof."

I thought he might be going crazy.

My mom once told me that when they first moved into our house, my dad would wake her saying he heard the devil walking on the roof. People were superstitious where he grew up in Brazil. His father, my grandfather, attended séances where they conjured spirits and tried to talk to them.

I slept okay those first few months, because I was sure my mother would return. I couldn't imagine she was gone forever. And I hadn't told anyone my birthday wish.

One night Dad came into my room, saying, "I can't take this. This is too painful. She has ripped apart my body and soul. I'd put a gun to my own head, I swear, if I didn't have you and Julie."

I hugged him.

"Dad," I said, "don't worry. She'll come back. Everything will be okay."

"My Jeremy," he said, sitting at the foot of my bed. "What would I do without you?"

Natalie set up a mattress for me on the floor of Stephen's bedroom, and I started spending nights there. My spot was next to his snake tank. Even though it smelled like wood chips and the red heat lamp stayed on all night, it was nice to be in a different place.

"When you're in this house, Jeremy," Natalie

said, "you're part of this family. You understand?"

"Yes, thank you," I said.

"Your father's going through a very rough time, and I want you here, happy and healthy."

When Stephen got back from camp, we swam in his pool and fished in the pond for sunfish and bass. Natalie took us fishing anywhere we wanted to go and cooked the best meals I'd tasted in months. At home our refrigerator was bare. There were moldy pieces of cheese that had been in there for weeks. My dad wasn't eating, and it seemed he didn't want anything to move or change. In the bathroom my mother's toothbrush was still in the same glass with my dad's and mine, and the special soap she used to wash her face was on top of a small towel by the sink. Her bathrobe was still behind their bedroom door. He hoped, like I did, that one day soon she'd return and everything would go back to the way it had been.

Not only was Stephen's refrigerator full of meat, bread, cheese, and fruit—and the cabinets loaded with chips and the freezer with ice cream—

Natalie made sure I ate and brushed my teeth and slept soundly.

Natalie told me, "Help yourself to anything. You're part of the family. Grab it and growl." The expression made me laugh whenever I heard it.

One night before Natalie went up the stairs to bed, she poked her head into the TV room where Stephen and I were sitting and reminded me that I was welcome to eat anything I wanted.

"Grab it and growl," she said.

"Okay, Natalie," Stephen said sarcastically, switching channels on the TV with the remote in his hand. Then he mimicked her in a high-pitched voice: "Grab it and growl."

"Oh, Stephen," Natalie said, and went up the stairs.

I turned to Stephen on the couch.

"You shouldn't treat your mom like that."

He didn't say anything.

I went to the kitchen and took a bag of chips from the cabinet, then returned to the TV room. Stephen was flipping through the channels. I ate a chip, looked at him, and growled. Then I laughed.

"You haven't asked my permission to eat those chips," he said, staring at the TV.

"Your mom said I could."

"So?"

"So."

"Yeah, well, she's not in charge—I am." He laughed and took the bag of chips from me. "When my dad's away, I'm in charge."

Stephen's uncle, Stanley, came over at least once a week. One night he brought lobsters for dinner that he'd trapped in Long Island Sound. It was the first time I ever ate lobster. Dipped in melted butter, it was sweet and delicious.

Natalie cleaned the dishes while Stanley sat back in his chair to smoke his pipe near the open window. Stephen and I were kicking a soccer ball around outside, and I came in to get a glass of water. When I passed the kitchen, I heard them talking, and I stopped by the sliding door to listen.

"I had to get him out of that house," Natalie was saying.

"Pretty bad, huh?" Stanley asked.

"His father is a wonderful man, but he's sick right now. He's not eating, and he cries all the time. The boy needs a stable home."

"You see him eat those lobsters?" Stanley asked chuckling. "Think he never ate a lobster before."

"I don't think he did," Natalie said. "His mother practically starved him. But in another sense they were so close. He and his mom were inseparable. He cried when she'd leave him here for overnights. That makes her leaving even harder to understand."

"That's tough."

"I'm just afraid he's holding it all in," Natalie said, wiping her hands on a dishrag. "He doesn't want to sleep alone in the guest room; he prefers to sleep on the floor in Stephen's room."

"You never bring it up?"

"How can I? We don't talk about that. I can hardly bear to think of what that woman did. I'm not going to judge her on leaving her husband—I know marriage can be tough—but a beautiful nine-year-old boy? I should have seen it coming. We went to the beach last summer. Phoebe was completely quiet, when usually she'd be jabbering like a blue jay. I think she made up her mind long before she actually left." Natalie dabbed her eyes with a napkin.

Stanley struck a match and lit his pipe.

"The boy will be fine," he said, puffing, a cloud of smoke around his face.

"I hope so."

"Boys are resilient. We convert our pain into achievements; we bury, press on."

Natalie threw a wet dishrag in Stanley's face.

"You really believe that?" she shouted. "Don't tell me you could say that with a straight face when Linda left you."

Tobacco ashes leaped out of his pipe and onto his lap.

"What?" he asked.

Natalie continued. "Bury and press on? Is that what you did when Dad left us?"

Stanley got up, and I was afraid I might be seen, so I ran back outside to join Stephen. I forgot that I was thirsty, but I left the room with a sick feeling in my gut.

I did spend some nights at home, but not many, especially since Dad started to go out some evenings. He apologized and prepared dinner for me ahead of time. He sat with me while I ate, then drove me to Stephen's.

"I'm going out with Jim Capella," he said one night. Jim was a teacher at the school where my dad taught. "We're going to a church in town where they have dances. It's like where single people meet."

As we drove down the dark road to Stephen's, my dad said, "When I heard my parents fighting, I was afraid they'd break up and I'd have no place to live. I just want you to know, Jeremy, I'm working hard on this. I'm going to make it. Your mother may be out of our lives, but you have nothing to fear. I will make sure we have a stable family again."

I knew that he meant replacing my mom.

Many nights I dreamed about my mom—that we were taking a nap together in the living room on a Sunday afternoon. My dreams seemed so real, as if the awake world were the nightmare. When I woke up, I'd try to go back to sleep and have the same dream again.

One night, sleeping in Stephen's room next to the snake tank, I had a dream that my mother and I were falling from the sky. We were trying to hold hands, but the air and the clouds kept us away from each other. Our fingertips nearly touched several times. We were headed for a big lake, or the ocean. I didn't know if we'd die or not, but I wasn't afraid. My mom kept repeating, "I never meant to hurt you, Jeremy. I'm so, so sorry. I am. I'm so sorry."

"It's okay, Mom," I said. "I knew you'd come back."

In my dream, I realize I can't see my mom's face. I look at her and it's just a blond woman with blue eyes, but barely a nose or cheeks or ears. It's as if she's out of focus.

• • •

I woke up, and as I lifted my head, I hit it on the bottom of the snake tank. The snake was coiled up the in the sawdust, looking at me. My shirt was soaked in sweat. I'd forgotten what my mother looked like. Even the sheets were damp, and I was shaking.

6. *The flowers I had planted, pruned, and weeded* with my mom—the day lilies, peonies, and lilies of the valley—were blooming. Every time I walked by the flower beds, I saw her standing with her cotton gloves and garden shears. Every object in the house had been touched by her, had some memory of her next to it, sitting on it, cleaning it, talking to it. I smelled her in the flowers, in the cut grass. In order to forget her, I had to shut them out too, which made me angry.

She's not even here and she's spoiling my favorite time of year.

Mrs. Kachele, our neighbor across the street and the widow of the old dairy farmer, had just had an operation on her hip. She couldn't get around, so my dad volunteered me to help her. It was nice to get out of the house, anyway.

I walked up the cement steps with her mail, past the jug where some paper wasps made their nest, through the creaky screen door to the kitchen. I kept her company at the kitchen table. She was eighty years old, so she had the stories that go with all those years. I pretended I was interested in what she said. Sometimes I was.

"When I met Andy—Mr. Kachele—this street was just a dirt path," she said, looking through old cake recipes she kept in a shoe box. "There were no cars or electricity when I was a girl. I went to school in a one-room schoolhouse, milked cows, cut hay by hand."

Another day Mrs. Kachele was in her wheelchair in the living room, by the big picture window facing the pond. She was hunched over the puzzles she liked to put together, take apart, and put together again. On the table next to her were a dozen prescription bottles.

"Jeremy, good of you to come again," Mrs. Kachele said, putting on her reading glasses. She pointed to a wooden chair with a needlepoint cushion. "Sit down."

"You tell me if it's none of my business," she continued in her crackly voice, gazing off at the pond, one lazy eye looking toward me. "But your father's getting thin. Is he eating?" She wiped the sweat from her forehead with a red-and-white-checkered dishcloth.

"Not much," I said.

"Tell me something. Are you in touch with your mother?"

"No," I said.

She continued staring at the pond, nodding.

"I remember your mom coming to see me before you were born. She said that she and your dad were expecting a girl, because that's what the doctors said. Your heartbeat was slow. But she insisted you'd be a boy. They put her in a pink room in the hospital. They were sure you'd be a girl."

Mrs. Kachele sighed. I leaned forward in my chair.

"I've known your parents a long time. Your dad wasn't easy all the time." She laughed. "When he lost his temper, we could hear him yelling all the way down the street. Well, your mom was right—you're a boy. Your parents had a Siamese cat, and when they brought you home from the hospital it jumped in your crib. Your dad thought it was jealous and wanted to scratch you. So he put it in a bag, went out in the backyard and shot it."

"He shot a cat?" I asked. I thought that maybe she was making it up. But how could she?

"Yes, your dad could be very angry. You don't remember?"

I shook my head.

Why is she telling me this?

"Dear, can you get me some iced tea to wash down these pills?" she asked.

I went to the kitchen. As I opened the refrigerator door to get the iced tea, I had a strange memory of my dad yelling at me because I'd finished the iced tea and forgotten to mix more. My mom came to my defense. "He's just a kid, Carl—he can barely reach the sink." But my dad wouldn't let up. "Stop defending him!" he yelled. "You're going to make him into a mama's boy."

I'd forgotten how angry he could get. I didn't want to remember.

I grabbed Mrs. Kachele's glass and poured it full.

"Thank you," she said when I returned. I stood by her, trying to find a polite way to leave.

Mrs. Kachele took a big swallow. "You hear about the time your dad shot the guy's tires?"

"No," I said, still standing.

"Your dad had a house in Bridgeport he rented out. The tenant wasn't paying the rent, so your father tried to kick him out. Then the tenant came to your house and threatened your mom. Your dad was out, but when he got home, the guy was still there. They had an argument, and your dad went to get his pistol, a Smith and Wesson. He walked outside and shot the guy's tires. When the cops came, they arrested your dad, because the car was on the street, on public property, and they took his pistol. We heard the shots, and Andy went over to see what was going on. Andy had to go downtown and bail him out."

"Do you want some more iced tea?" I asked. Her glass was almost empty again.

"No," she said, "that'll be fine."

I started to walk away.

"Will I see you tomorrow?" she asked. "I don't expect to see you every day, but I have to say I've grown used to it."

I nodded.

As I walked down the cement steps, past the ceramic jug with the paper wasp nest, past the peonies, I got light-headed and dizzy. I could barely remember what my dad was like before my mom left. *It wasn't that long ago.*

Thunderheads rumbled over the hill.

I felt sick, and the dirt-sweet smell of the flowers

made me sicker. I held my head. The sky turned yellow-green, then gray. I lay on our lawn across the street from Mrs. Kachele's house, and soon I felt raindrops on my face. Cooler and fresher air came with the rain. The sky opened up and the rain drenched me.

7. *Sometimes when I looked at the paintings* I was making that summer and compared them to ones I had made before she left, I thought the old ones were definitely better. I was wasting my time now. I wasn't an artist like my mom used to say. She used to tell me I'd be famous. This new stuff was awful. But on other days I thought, *No, the newer pictures are better. I am better off without her.*

But I didn't want to be better off without her. My sister, Julie, sometimes said to me, "Life isn't all about what you want, Jeremy." Maybe she was right.

The first day of school, my dad forgot to pack my lunch. It used to just appear on the kitchen counter. The empty feeling came back. The feeling that there were more things I'd taken for granted that could never be replaced.

Stop whining. Get a grip.

I kept reminding myself that I liked school. I tried to be in a good mood on the bus. I liked school.

No one brought it up in first period. They whispered about how Dan had grown a foot taller, how Mike had broken his arm in a car accident. There were two new girls, pretty twin sisters, so they got lots of attention. I was thinking maybe no one had heard about my parents' divorce.

It's not all about you, I could hear Julie say.

At lunch some of the cool kids were looking at me strangely. Mike invited me to eat at their table.

"Where's your lunch, Jeremy?" he asked.

"Yeah," Ben said, "where's the brown bag?"

I shrugged.

"Well, here," Mike said, "take my fries." He grabbed a handful of fries and put them on his tray for me. Other boys in the group sat down, each adding something to the tray: a pickle, a hot dog, a soda. Stephen sat down at the end of the table, smiling.

Mike leaned over.

"I heard about your parents," he said. "That sucks."

And that was it. Everyone knew, but they didn't say another word. All afternoon I went through the motions, going from class to class, not wanting to be there. In my mind I was at my camp in the woods, preparing my shelter for the night.

Then I remembered.

Evan.

I hadn't thought much about him that summer. As soon as I got to school, the fear crept in. He was probably just around the corner in the hall waiting to trip me. My face turned red as the thought I'd been avoiding all summer came into my head:

Is he living with my mom?

Eventually, I learned that Evan visited his dad on Sundays. One kid, Joe, said he'd even gone with Evan one weekend to hang out with Evan's father.

"What did you do?" I asked Joe.

"We tossed the ball around in a park."

"Where?"

"Down in Bridgeport."

"Was there a woman there?"

"Yeah, she was tossing the ball too, but she couldn't throw."

"Oh, God!" I said.

Sundays.

My mom played catch?

I don't know how I avoided Evan the first two weeks, but somehow I managed it. Then one day, he stopped me in the hall. I was whistling a song, thinking of the woods. He came up behind me and tapped me on the shoulder.

"You think other people want to hear your dumb whistling?" he said. "People keep telling you to stop being a dick, but you never listen."

"You're a dick," I said to him.

Kids surrounded us in the hall.

"Get him, Jeremy," one said, and laughed.

"Your mom's a weirdo," Evan said. "I guess it runs in the family."

I ran toward him and tackled him to the floor. The carpeted floor was harder than I imagined, but I was just thinking about how I wanted to hurt him really badly. Evan was on top of me, and I could hear Stephen in the background cheering me on. I got Evan in a headlock, and that's when Stephen bodychecked him and Mr. Hale, our history teacher, came out of his classroom.

"Your mother's a slut!" Evan screamed.

I wiped the sweat off my face.

"Boys! Stop this!" Mr. Hale said, looking very serious. "The three of you! Come with me."

He took us straight to the principal's office.

We sat quietly in the office. I could hear Mr. Mendel, the principal, on the phone through his office door.

As I sat there, I worked on my strategy. I would apologize, and Mr. Mendel would take pity on me.

When he called me in, I sat down in the chair

opposite Mr. Mendel's desk. He was a big round man. I looked down at my shaking knees.

"Don't think just because you're a good student you can get away with this behavior," he said. "Fighting in my school?"

"I'm sorry, Mr. Mendel—"

"Jeremy," he interrupted, leaning back in his chair, his big belly rising, "I'm disappointed. Evan and Stephen—I expect this from them. But you?"

"You don't understand."

"If I had a nickel for every time I heard that from a student, I'd be a billionaire. You think I don't understand? Try being an overweight kid. You can't give in to the teasing. What's happening at home doesn't give you a free ticket to act out. I don't care what's happening in your life. You're better than that."

"I'm sorry, Mr. Mendel," I repeated.

The principal tightened his lips. As he lifted his head, the wattles under his chin straightened. He had two tufts of reddish hair on either side of his mouth that made him look like a walrus.

"My advice to you is stay away from Evan. Don't talk to him. Don't look at him. If he comes up to you, walk the other way. If he hits you in the back, come to me, or take care of it somewhere else. If I hear you're in another fight in my school, I'll expel all three of you. Do you hear me? We're not in the babysitting business."

"Yes, sir," I said. I'd never said "yes, sir" to anyone.

"Get out of here," he said. "I don't ever want to see you in this office again." He leaned forward and grabbed a toothpick out of a penguin-shaped mug. "Send in Stephen."

Later that day, I saw Stephen at his locker.

"Can I come over today?" I asked.

"Sure. Take the bus to my house, but I won't be there until four."

"Why?"

"I got two days' detention."

"What?"

"Mendelephant strikes again."

"Thanks, Stephen. You didn't have to . . . get into my fight."

"No problem, man," he said, chewing on a pen cap. "It's my pleasure."

I avoided Evan like Mendel said. It wasn't hard because we didn't have any classes in common.

Out of sight, out of mind, I could hear my father say.

But Evan was seeing my mom and I wasn't—and that was something I couldn't get out of my head.

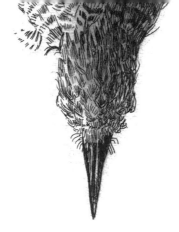

8. When the air got crisper and the leaves changed color, soccer season began. My dad was our coach. On the first day of practice, we gathered in front of the goal for his opening-day speech. With a black whistle on a string around his neck and a checkered ball in his hand, he began.

"I come from Brazil," he said. "You can hear my accent, eh?" They all nodded. "In Brazil, soccer is a game played by every boy." There was one girl on our team, named Florence. He gave her a wink and tossed the ball to her. "You know what I mean?" he said.

She threw the ball back at him.

"It's a simple game, played by poor kids on the streets. You don't need shin pads or cleats. You don't need anything but a ball. We didn't have nice leather soccer balls—we played barefoot with whatever ball we could find. That's how we developed our skills."

"Barefoot?" one of the kids asked.

"You don't believe me?" my dad asked.

The boy shook his head.

My dad took off his cleats and socks and juggled the ball barefoot, bouncing it off his chest and knees, head and feet. Then he kicked the ball over our heads into the goal. Everyone was amazed. *That's my dad!* I wanted to shout.

"Where I come from, soccer is not a sport, but a religion."

I'd heard this speech before, but this time was like it was the first time. My dad was animated, and his frown had turned into an energetic smile. I'd seen so many different people in him; I hoped this was the real one.

He motioned for everyone to get up. Then he got the ball from the goal and began dribbling around us barefoot while continuing to talk.

"I don't understand games where you touch the

ball with your hands." He kicked the ball through my legs. "In soccer you use your whole body to move the ball." He ran into a pack of five kids, lobbing the ball over their heads with his feet. "Your head," he said, demonstrating, "your chest . . . your legs . . . everything *except* your hands. Only the goalkeeper can use his hands."

He didn't hold back because we were ten years old. My dad played hard. He yelled and swore. They liked that he swore.

"I'm just a sailor," he said, dribbling the ball between their legs. "I have a sailor's mouth."

He smiled and laughed, and even rolled in the green grass, playing barefoot like he did when he was a boy.

Some kids tried to trip him as he showed off. A few stepped on his bare feet with their cleats. He kicked the ball at them so hard, it knocked them over. That fall, my father was one of us, and he earned the team's respect.

We had a good season, more wins than losses. We

played our games on Saturday mornings, sometimes Sundays. On game days, I helped my dad cut oranges into wedges for halftime.

My father looked healthy. He was tan from being outside, and he looked stronger, like Uncle John. We started taking long walks in the woods again, even to some of the places we used to go with my mom. On weekend afternoons, after soccer games, we went into the backyard to cut and split wood for the woodstove. My dad worked and sweated and smelled of sawdust, and in the evenings he read. On rainy October nights he talked about his childhood or his sailing days.

"In the rainy season everything filled up with water. It was like this rain falling now, a tropical rain. It fell so hard everything would shake. I spent rainy days at my grandmother Alcides's house. The house had a dirt floor. She'd give me a cup of coffee with lots of sugar." He laughed. "I wasn't allowed to drink coffee at home."

Word spread through school about how cool my

dad was, that he "swore like a sailor" and could dribble the ball like no one they'd ever seen.

I liked soccer, but sometimes I felt my dad's disappointment at the fact that I played goalie.

"Soccer for me was always about scoring," my dad said one night at dinner. "Don't you want to get out of the goal and play?"

I shrugged my shoulders. I wanted him to be proud of me, but I was afraid I wasn't good enough to score a goal.

Before practice one day he sat us down in front of the goal for a speech.

"My position was striker," he began. "I liked to score goals. Sometimes I was a little selfish, because I liked the feeling of running with the ball. But the most important rule in play is that you can't play the game all by yourself. No matter how good you are, this is a team sport. Passing is essential. We call it giving and receiving. Give and go. Humans are gregarious animals—that means we need others to survive. We're not in this alone."

He pulled a ball toward himself and began juggling it with his feet.

"The Brazilian team is a passing team," he said, his voice excited. "They win the World Cup with skill and beauty—and passing. Not by pushing and driving alone to the goal. So today, and for the rest of the season, we're going to work on passing."

We all stood up and played.

The team did pass, and toward the end of the season we took a big school bus, driven by my dad, to the regional championship.

Late in the second half of the championship game we were down one goal. There were only a few minutes left, and we had a corner kick.

"Everybody up the field," my dad yelled. "Everybody!" He blew his whistle. "You too, Jeremy!"

I pointed to myself standing in the goal and gave a questioning look. My dad waved his hand. I began to run upfield. I was running alone, past midfield, crossing line after white line, into offensive territory, to the other team's penalty box. As I passed each line, I felt more and more excited, exhilarated, like I was taking charge and risking everything at the same time.

"This is our last chance to score!" my father yelled to the team. But I felt like he was yelling to me. "I want everyone in there," he added.

The corner kick was up. I stood outside the pack on the far side of the goal. The ball came high, right toward my head. Or would it land at my feet?

I ran at the ball. All the other players pivoted on their feet. I was in perfect position to head the ball into the corner of the net. The ball flew over the fullbacks, and I connected with it. It launched off my head over the goalie's fingertips and sent the white rope net up and out as the ball hit it.

The game was tied.

My father ran out in the field and opened his arms.

"The goalie scores a goal!" he said hugging me, and I saw tears in his eyes. "See what happens when you step out, Jeremy!" he said hugging me. "When you work like a team!"

We didn't win the game—I let a goal in during sudden-death overtime—but it was still our best game of the season.

Soccer season was good for both my dad and me, but it came to an end. The winds became stronger and colder. Winter was on its way.

9. Thanksgiving was the first family holiday without my mom. We spent it at Uncle John's, like we always did, with Aunt Janice and my cousins, Janeen, Michele, and Jill.

We had the same turkey dinner we had every year, with Aunt Janice's cranberry sauce, stuffing, butternut squash, sweet potatoes, mashed potatoes, creamed spinach, apple pie, and pumpkin pie. I didn't feel my mom's absence, because the table was full of family. Even Julie was there, and I wondered where she'd been lately.

She had a boyfriend now, named Anthony. My dad and I knew that she used her bedroom window like a door. We hardly ever saw her coming or going.

"How are things?" my aunt asked Julie.

Julie shrugged her shoulders.

"I'd like to know myself," my dad said, joking. "The only three words I've heard out of her in the last few months are 'see you later.'"

Everyone laughed. Even my cousins.

"*Dad*," Julie said, sounding embarrassed.

"Yeah," I said, "Julie has a boyfriend."

"Shut up, Jeremy."

I knew she spent a lot of time at Carey's house, like I did at Stephen's, but I was wondering about something else.

Is she seeing Mom?

"The girl has her own car now," Uncle John said. "Car equals freedom."

"Right," Dad said.

Aunt Janice changed the subject.

"Let's say grace," she said. We all held hands, and Aunt Janice began. "Grant us the serenity to accept the things we cannot change, the courage to change the things we can, and the wisdom to know the difference. God, thank you for this bountiful dinner, and for our family here today. We all need each other, especially on this holiday of giving thanks."

"Well," my dad said. "Amen."

I ate until I couldn't move. Janeen and my sister went upstairs, I guessed to talk about boys, and my older cousin, Michele, played the piano. When it was dark, we watched a Godzilla movie on TV by the warm woodstove. I used Uncle John's dog, Rusty, as a foot rest. When I went into the kitchen to get some ice cream, I ran into Julie making tea.

"Are you seeing Mom?" I asked.

"No," she said.

"Really?"

"Look, Jeremy, it's none of your business."

"I'll take that as a yes," I said. "You're lying."

"Jeremy."

"'Jeremy,' what?"

"Look, it's just not a good time to talk about it."

Aunt Janice walked into the kitchen.

I couldn't begin to imagine what it would be like to see my mom. If I saw her, I'd think she was a ghost. I didn't really believe she existed anymore.

Dad and Julie left that evening, but I had fallen asleep on the couch by the woodstove and my dad let me sleep.

When Uncle John came downstairs early the next morning, Rusty lifted her spotted head and shook her body, head to tail, jangling her collar. It was still before dawn and dark in the house. My uncle filled the woodstove and blew on the embers until the new wood caught fire. Then he made a pot of coffee. I got out from under the warm wool blanket, right where I'd fallen asleep with all my clothes on, and went into the kitchen.

"Sleep well?" he asked. He was wearing glasses.

"Yeah," I said.

"Should be a good day," Uncle John said looking out the window. "No breeze, light frost. Just above freezing."

The first bird of the morning hopped onto the bird feeder, a chickadee.

Uncle John put two slices of toast in front of me

along with a dish of butter and some jam. He opened the door to walk out and get the newspaper, and a cold breeze brushed my feet.

"We'll be back by breakfast," he said, looking out the window at the yard. It was still dark. "But you might want to eat something now."

"Where are we going?" I asked.

"Hunting."

I'd been out enough times with Uncle John to know that he sometimes lost track of time and that I'd better eat as much as I could while I had the chance. I buttered my toast.

"I know you don't like coffee," he said, "so I made you some hot chocolate." He poured hot water and the powdered mix into a traveling mug. He grabbed his gun, and Rusty followed us into the garage, where she jumped up in the passenger seat next to me.

"There's good cover for grouse where we're going," Uncle John said, sipping coffee out of his thermos. "Ten years ago it was all open, with cattle grazing, the dairy farm still operating. The old farmer was still alive. It's all cedar trees now, multiflora rose, and bittersweet. The kids of the farmer are looking to sell it. If they build houses, all the birds will disappear. Their habitat will be gone. Grouse like the thickest cover." He patted the dog on her brown and white head. "That's your job, Rusty," he said. "Find them and flush them."

The road wound back and forth though the leafless trees. As the road got narrower, the land opened up. There were fewer trees and more fields. We came to a red barn by the side of the road. My uncle pulled off and parked the truck.

The sun was up, and it was warm enough now that I didn't have to wear a wool cap. Uncle John grabbed his gun and a few shot out of a box and put them in the pocket of his hunting jacket. When he pulled his hand out of the jacket pocket, a handful of feathers came with it. Rusty sniffed the feathers as they floated to the ground.

"That's it, girl," Uncle John said. "That's what we're after."

He handed me an orange safety vest to put on, and we followed a trail beside the barn through the brambles. Uncle John and Rusty moved—through the tall, dry grass; over dead leaves, lichen-covered boulders, and stone walls; by the hickory trees—as one. Rusty seemed to be led by her nose, my uncle by his eyes. I did all I could to keep up.

Suddenly Uncle John stopped. Rusty was on point about ten yards in front of us. A grouse burst into the air. I heard the *whooph* of its feathers. Uncle John swung his gun, aimed, and shot.

POW.

The grouse cartwheeled to the ground.

He dressed the bird by a small stream, cutting its breast and cleaning out the guts. He plucked the bird, and I shoved a few feathers in my pocket.

10. A week later, Dad suggested we go to Grady's Tree Farm to pick out a Christmas tree. At the last minute Julie decided to come with us. She sat in the passenger seat wearing a white down jacket with a fur collar.

"You sure you want to wear that, Julie?" Dad asked as he got in the car. "It might get dirty."

"I think I'm old enough to dress myself," Julie responded.

"You buy that thing?" I asked.

"What do you think? I got a job at the mall making my own money. Jesus, if I'd known I was going to get the third degree, I would've stayed home."

"Don't do us any favors," I said.

Julie huffed and grabbed the handle on the passenger-side door, like she was getting out.

My dad took her by the arm.

"Don't listen to Jeremy," he said. "I want you here."

The parking lot at the tree farm was full, and families of all kinds were tying trees to the roof racks of their cars. A big field of Christmas trees stood in front of us. A man in overalls handed my father a saw with a red handle.

"I like that one," Julie said, pointing, not ten yards down the path.

"That's no good," I said. "It's a white pine."

"Dad, please tell Jeremy to shut up."

"Well, firs and spruces make better Christmas trees," my dad agreed. "The branches on pines are flimsy. You can't hang ornaments on them."

"Fine," she said. "If you don't want my opinion, why'd you ask me to come?"

"I know why she's being like this," I said out loud. "Because she's seeing Mom. You're taking her side, aren't you?"

"Jeremy," my dad said. "We hardly get to see your sister. Why don't you try and be nice?"

My dad took the saw and started to cut down the pine.

"Why are you doing that, Dad?" I asked. "Don't let her have her way that easily."

"Jeremy," my dad stopped. "I'm not going to tell you again."

"But why are you taking her side?"

"You get everything you want," Julie said. "Dad's practically your slave. The living room's a shrine to your paintings. Is there a picture of me anywhere?"

Julie turned and started walking back to the car.

"Jeremy!" my father shouted. He put down the saw, shook his fist and gave me a threatening look. I remembered suddenly the dad I had known before my mom left. He'd been too weak to get angry after she left, but now he was getting his strength back, and his anger was showing.

"Apologize right now. She's the only sister you have."

"Thank God," I said. But I don't think he heard me, because if he did, he would have gotten angrier.

"Julie!" my dad said. "Come back here!"

She turned around.

"Jeremy!" my dad said.

"Okay. I'm sorry." Then I stuck my tongue out at him when he wasn't looking.

We all walked back to the half-cut tree.

"You need each other," my dad said. "You may not realize it now, but you will."

That was it. The saw continued its path through the tree. I smelled the strong pine smell from the branches and the resin. It was a nice tree. I felt bad for starting a fight.

Julie walked away.

"Not so fast," Dad said. "You picked it. You can help carry it. Take off that white coat before you get tree sap on it." Julie handed Dad the coat. She put her hand on one of the lower branches. I grabbed another, and we started to drag the tree to the car. We felt the sap sticking to our fingers.

The men in the parking lot tied the tree to the roof of our car with twine. A woman came up to collect the money for the tree. She was about my dad's age, with curly red hair, freckles, and light white skin. For a second, standing next to each other, they almost looked like a couple. They talked for a bit about this and that, and I saw the way the woman smiled at my father, a familiar warm smile.

We put up the tree in a different corner of the living room than usual. Dad struggled, trying to get the tree to stand up straight in the old tree stand with its rusted screws. We dressed the tree with white lights and a few colored glass ornaments. The old boxes of ornaments we kept in the basement were like an awful box of memories. Julie and I found the ones we'd made at school over the years and hung them in the back. The colorful ceramic bears and penguins we had made with our mom—those stayed in the box.

11. *"Time heals,"* my father began to say almost daily. He was snapping out of it. I was snapping out of it too, but slowly. Sometimes a memory leaked in—the trip we took skiing at Mohawk Mountain, or my mom cooking hard-boiled eggs on the stove—and I felt the familiar hope that she might return. Since the day she left, I hadn't received a note or a call or any reason for me to think she remembered me.

On a beautiful day in early December, I walked outside and could have sworn she was there next to me. We were deciding where we were going to hike. She was preparing some things in a backpack to bring along, some apples, raisins, a bottle of water. I shook my head. *Remember. Even on the best days they were fighting.* They fought about what road to take, who forgot to fill the gas tank. I wondered if she fought with Paul Sullivan, with her new family. I knew things couldn't be perfect all the time.

Does she regret leaving?

And one night as I lay in bed, I had the thought of my mom spending Christmas with Evan and his younger sister. It came on like a fever, a rush of warm heat that kept me up all night, made my head pound into the pillow. I wished there was a way to take that piece of my brain out and smash it. But no matter how I tried to kill it, the fantasy reemerged, the flawless mother with my worst enemy.

Two weeks before Christmas vacation I got strange news.

Evan's spine was deformed; he'd been in and out seeing back specialists all term. I remembered the scoliosis tests, where the nurse tells you to bend over and touch your toes while she runs her cold fingers along your spine under your shirt. I remembered seeing the poster in her office of a girl with a normal spine next to a girl with a spine that was curved. Word in the halls was that Evan would be operated on after Christmas.

Stephen said he'd gotten what was coming. I tried hard not to find happiness in the news.

I felt a lump grow in my throat as I thought how scared Evan must be. I remembered when a girl in our school had died of leukemia. It was like a wild animal had come into the school and killed her, a totally random accident. What were the chances that you might be next? What if you just happened to be standing by the front doors when the animal came in and grabbed you by the neck? What if I were Evan, and I had the curved spine? I would be scared. But then I thought, if I ever got that sick, maybe my mom would find out, and feel sorry for me, and come back just to take care of me. When Evan came out of his operation to straighten his spine, I wondered if my mom would sit by his bed and take care of him.

The next day, reaching for a warm pair of wool socks deep in my dresser drawer, I came across the pieces of the plate I'd hidden the night my parents came home from the dinner at Josh's. I'd forgotten all about them.

I took them down to my dad's workbench in the basement, and with some super glue, I put the plate back
together. Then, don't ask me why, I blurted out a prayer
for Evan, even though I hated him so much. My mom
had told me to pray for my enemies—that it would help
the "healing." She was right; the prayer made some of
the hate go away. When the glue dried, I put the plate
back at the bottom of my sock drawer.

Maybe my dad was right and time did heal. Months
before, I couldn't have gone near those pieces of the
plate. But time passing also meant letting go. My dad
was no longer waiting for my mom to come back; he was
moving forward. And months before now, I could never
have imagined I'd ever feel sorry for Evan, let alone pray
for him. Life seemed like a bunch of coincidences strung
together, and we were living between them.

One night over dinner, my dad said, "You remember that woman at the tree farm?"

"What woman?" I asked.

"You know—she helped us put the Christmas tree
on the car, and she took the money?"

It hadn't been that long since we'd gotten the tree. It now stood lit up in the corner of the living room. I thought back to that day. *Yeah, I remember.* She was the woman who had smiled at my dad.

"What about her?"

"Well, I invited her for dinner tomorrow."

I guess I should have seen it coming. The signs were there. He spent more nights out and was even talking on the phone now and then. My dad never used the phone except to make plans. But what was odd was that I'd been thinking of the tree woman lately too, and now she was coming over to the house.

"Tomorrow is the winter solstice," Dad said, changing the subject, "the shortest day of the year. Tonight is supposed to be very cold. The pond should be frozen. Maybe we'll go skating on Saturday."

I stared at my plate and didn't know whether to be angry or happy.

The next day, my dad asked Julie if she'd stay for dinner instead of going to Carey's house.

"But, Dad," Julie said, "you never ask me to stay for dinner."

"I know, but this night is different."

"Why?"

"I have someone coming over I want you to meet." He took out his handkerchief to wipe his nose. I thought he was going to cry.

"Yeah, Dad, sure," Julie said. "I have to go. See you later."

"She's coming over at seven," Dad shouted. "Make sure you're here."

I picked up the kitchen phone.

"Hi, Natalie, is Stephen there?"

"Yeah," she said. "Hang on."

"Hey, Stephen," I said when he got on the phone, "I think the pond will be frozen enough to skate tomorrow." I was talking about the pond near his house. "Let's get a hockey game together."

"Sure."

"And maybe I'll come over for dinner tonight," I added, loudly enough for my dad to hear me.

"Sure," Stephen said.

"Okay, well . . . but I might need a ride."

"Sure no problem, Natalie will come get you."

"Um, okay, I'll let you know."

I hung up the phone.

"Jeremy," my dad said from the next room, "you're not going to dinner at Stephen's tonight."

"Why?"

"Because I have a guest coming for dinner I want you to meet."

"Why do I have to be here?"

"Because I said so."

"Blah blah, 'said so,'" I said, parroting him. "Tell me what 'said so' means and I'll stay."

"'Said so' means that I'm your father, and what I say goes," he said, raising his voice.

I called Stephen and canceled our plans.

Susan came just after dark. At first, she didn't go any farther than the laundry room. Through the crack at the door hinges, I thought I saw my dad give her a kiss. Her cheeks were reddish from the wind and cold.

She took off her black shoes, left them neatly by the door, and walked in with her socks on. No shoes! She was making herself right at home. She smelled different from our house, a perfume smell.

She brought all the fixings for dinner in plastic containers and set them on the kitchen counter.

"Julie," my dad said, "this is Susan."

"Hi, nice to meet you," she said, and shook her hand.

"And this is Jeremy."

"Hi, Jeremy," Susan said. She put out her hand for me to shake. It was warm and soft, like her voice.

"Well," my dad said, "why don't you sit in the living room while I heat up dinner?" Dad rummaged around in the kitchen, pulling out pots to heat up the food.

I followed Julie and Susan to the living room. They sat next to each other on the couch, and I sat in a chair nearby. Julie's legs were folded under her, and Susan sat up straight with her legs together.

"So, you work at the tree farm?" Julie asked.

"No, actually, I'm in market research."

"What were you doing at the tree farm?" I asked.

"My dad and mom own the farm," she said. "I grew up there. I help out during the holidays. We prune the trees in summer. It gets me out; I like it. It's my way of reconnecting."

"Reconnecting?" Julie asked.

"With nature," Susan said. "With my parents."

"What did you say you did?" Julie asked.

"Market research."

"What's that?" I asked.

"Well, I have clients, like Hershey, and—"

"You mean the chocolate company?" Julie interrupted.

"Yes. If Hershey comes out with a new product—like, I don't know, a chocolate bar with strawberry flavor—we do tests, research, to see how the product will do in the marketplace."

"How do you do that?"

"We do surveys."

"Like," Julie started, "you mean the kind in the mall where people get paid to eat something and tell them what they think of it? Oh my God, that's so cool!"

"I wouldn't call it cool," Susan said, "but it's okay."

Dad walked in.

"Dinner ready?" Susan asked.

"Does that mean you get free chocolate?" I asked.

"I get more free chocolate than I can eat," Susan said.

I watched her face as she talked. I thought she was a bird, but couldn't place what kind. Her beak was sharp, her face was round. I wasn't sure. She was foreign, freckled. *A starling, maybe?* My dad smiled. Even if I didn't like Susan, what could I do?

"I think we should sit down and eat," Dad said.

We sat in our usual places at the kitchen table, with Susan sitting by the window where my mom used to sit. The food was good, pork chops with mashed potatoes.

"Your dad told me you're working in the mall," Susan said to Julie.

"Yeah, I work in a jewelry store. You know, but it's not nice jewelry."

"That sounds like fun," Susan said, then turned to me. "And you, Jeremy? You're a painter?"

"I like to draw," I said.

"I can see." She looked at the bookshelves where a few of my drawings were leaning against the books. "You're very talented."

"Yeah," Julie said. "But it's a little annoying that there's so much of his stuff in this room."

I rolled my eyes.

"Jeremy," my dad said, "say thank you for the compliment."

"Thanks," I said quietly.

I lay awake in bed after Susan left, thinking about how things might change now. A winter wind was shaking the trees. The bare branches were rattling like icicles, and a cold, bluish moon was lighting up the ground.

• • •

Stephen called me the next morning. "Come over. We're getting a hockey game together."

"Okay, I'll try and get a ride. See you soon."

I hung up the phone in the kitchen and ran to Julie's room.

"Julie," I said, "can you please give me a ride to Stephen's?"

"I'm not a taxi, Jeremy."

"I know, but Dad and I were supposed to go skating, and now he's got that woman coming back again. I don't want to be here."

"Okay, chill."

I ran down to the basement, grabbed my skates, and loaded Julie's car with my gloves, down jacket, and hockey stick.

"Are you ready?" I asked Julie, returning to her room.

"Hold on a second. Let me get my own stuff together. I'm going over to Carey's."

Julie and I walked out the door toward her car when we heard my dad's voice.

"Wait a minute—where are you two going?"

"I'm taking Jeremy to Stephen's," Julie said, turning to face my father, who stood by the open screen door. "Then Carey and I are going out."

"Well," he said, "I thought *we* were going skating."

Julie and I kept walking.

"Bye, Dad," I said.

"All right. Have fun."

I got in Julie's red Volkswagen Bug and shut the door. The car was running and already warm. A light snow started to fall.

We were halfway to Stephen's before Julie spoke. She took out a cigarette and lit it.

"Julie," I said. "I didn't know you smoked."

"There's a lot of things you don't know about me," she said. "Or about life for that matter."

"Those things will kill you."

Julie shrugged her shoulders. Her window was open a crack to let the smoke out. It was a very cold day, but the old heater in the Volkswagen worked well. The air from the heater reminded me of our grandfather. It still smelled like him. I got a tingling chill up my neck, like you get when you think someone dead is standing in the room with you.

"Jeremy, you've got to be realistic about this. I want you to know, Dad's not going to stay alone the rest of his life."

"Fine. I don't have to like it. Do I?"

"No, but I think you'd better give it a chance, because fighting it's not going to help you."

"Why not?"

"'Cause if Dad's unhappy, you will be too. I know you're used to getting your way, but it's not going to happen like that now."

"We'll see," I said.

"At least you have friends," Julie said. "All that Dad has had in the last few months, besides you and me, is work."

Julie pulled into Stephen's driveway. The gravel made a crunching sound under the tires.

"We're lucky in a way," Julie said. "We get out of the house. I go to Carey's; you go to Stephen's. Dad's stuck there with all those memories. Every time I pick up a spoon I think of what things were like before, how everything changed so much, all of a sudden."

"Is that why you're never home?"

"Maybe," Julie said.

Stephen ran toward Julie's car, swinging his hockey stick. Julie rolled down her window. "Get the hell away from my car," she yelled, half joking.

I guess Dad was right. I do need Julie.

12. *That Sunday it started snowing about midday.* The snow fell lightly and then more heavily through the night. Every hour or so before I went to bed I turned on the outside light by the porch to make sure the snow was still falling. Snowfall like this felt like a dream come true! It just kept coming down. With any luck school would be canceled.

Before falling asleep that night I said a prayer, and then I thought about Susan and my dad. I didn't really want my dad to be alone, but at the same time I wasn't ready to have a new person in our house. Still, I knew having Susan around couldn't hurt as much as the early days after my mom left, when I missed her so much I could hardly breathe, dreaming while not asleep of seeing her or speaking with her again.

I looked out the window to make sure the snow was still falling. I saw the light from Julie's bedroom window cast on the snow.

She's still awake.

I thought about going downstairs to talk to her. How did Julie feel about all this? I didn't know how to ask her. I was just glad to know she was home.

I slept well that night, comforted by the gentle sound of falling snow blowing against the window.

We woke in the morning, and Dad took the yardstick out on the porch to measure the snow. "We haven't had a storm this big in ten years," he said. "Twenty-one inches. The biggest storm of your life, Jeremy."

Julie, my dad, and I sat around the kitchen radio. We knew school would be canceled, but we had to listen to the radio for confirmation.

"The following schools are closed," the radio voice said. *"Abbot Tech, Ansonia, Bethel, Bridgeport, Beacon Falls, Canaan, Danbury, Darien, Derby, Easton . . ."*

"Yes!" Julie exclaimed. "I don't have to face Ms. Bitch today."

"Julie," my dad said, "don't talk about your teachers that way."

"But that's her name," Julie insisted.

I laughed. "It is, Dad," I put in. "It's Ms. Beech."

"That language. Where do you pick it up?"

"From you, Dad," Julie said.

"Oh, I guess that's true," he confessed. "Sailor's mouth."

Julie's red Volkswagen Beetle sat buried under several feet of drifted snow in our driveway. She made us pancakes and put them on the kitchen table with pats of butter between them.

"I'm glad for the snow," my dad said, forking pancakes onto his plate. "Sailors never wish for storms at sea. But if it takes a storm to get this family together, then that's what it takes." He shrugged.

We laughed a little because it was true.

• • •

After breakfast, Julie and I walked down to the pond with shovels, skates, and hockey sticks. People from the neighborhood were already shoveling out a small rink, and had brought a few bales of hay from the barn to use as benches. As the roads were plowed, cars pulled up with people from different parts of town. A small hockey game formed. We whizzed around, laughing, falling, and holding hands. I ended up with black and blue marks on my arms and legs.

"What do you think of that woman Dad's hanging around with?" I said to Julie when we stopped to rest.

"You mean Susan?" Julie asked.

"Yeah."

We slid our skates back and forth on the ice.

"It's probably for the best," Julie said.

"Maybe for Dad, but what about me?"

"Dad told me she's spending Christmas Eve with us."

"Dad told you that?"

"Yeah."

I got up and grabbed my hockey stick.

"Why didn't he tell me?"

I skated off toward the center of the pond, slapping my stick on the ice, hoping the whole thing would shatter.

Sure enough, a week later, the afternoon of Christmas Eve, Susan came over carrying a blue and white gym bag and a tray of food wrapped in tin foil. She handed the tray to my father and took the gym bag upstairs to my dad's bedroom.

A fire was already burning in the fireplace. I cornered my dad in the kitchen. He was putting the tray of food in the oven.

"Why is she here?" I asked.

"Because," he said, giving me a look, "she makes me feel better."

The timer went off by the stove. *Bzzzzzzz.*

Susan came into the kitchen. She had changed into a red dress.

"How's the lasagna?" she asked.

I stood by the stove. My dad acted like Susan was

part of the family, like it was normal that she had just appeared in our kitchen with a lasagna. It made me angry. How did she know lasagna was my favorite?

"Do you want to set the table for dinner?" Dad asked me.

"No," I said. I went upstairs and sat at my desk to work on a drawing of a starling that I'd started earlier. Drawing made me feel better. When I'd completed it I went back downstairs.

I didn't recognize the kitchen table. It had a red tablecloth on it and cloth napkins. There were two sets of forks, a knife, and a spoon at each place, and two red candles in silver holders. In the center of the table was a poinsettia. On the shelf behind the table, where the telephone usually was and where my dad kept his bills, was a row of nutcrackers, toy soldiers, and Santa figurines. None of them were ours.

She must have brought them in when I was up in my room drawing. We never gave Christmas this much fuss before.

Susan lit the candles. They smelled like cinnamon.

Julie, Dad, and I sat in our usual spots, while Susan brought out the hot tray of lasagna. Then she sat by the window, in the place where my mom used to sit.

My mouth watered with hunger, and I pressed my lips together and kept swallowing. Susan took a spatula and a knife and cut a square of lasagna for my plate. I cut into the little golden brown domes where the cheese had melted and bubbled up and shoved the piece in my mouth. It was delicious. Mom had never cooked like this.

I laughed a little because I didn't know what else to do. I felt guilty for enjoying Susan's lasagna—but it was so good! My laugh sounded like a cough, though, and no one really noticed.

After dinner it was time to open presents. We always opened presents on Christmas Eve.

We sat by the tree. There were actually presents under the tree. Where had they come from?

"I like the tree," Susan said, staring at it. "I like white pines. They're soft and they don't hold ornaments well, but they're beautiful—plus they smell nice."

"Thank you," Julie said.

Susan walked over to the tree and grabbed a gift. She handed it to me, and I tore off the wrapping paper. The gift was a set of fifty colored pencils. I twisted my face, trying not to smile, but a grin slowly spread across my face.

"I think he likes it," Julie said, giving me a look.

"I do," I said. "I really do. Thank you."

"Look under the box," Susan said. "That's from your father and me, both."

There was an envelope with a thin course booklet inside that listed classes at Silvermine Art School. One of the classes was highlighted: BEGINNER DRAWING 116: TAUGHT BY JACK INGRAM.

"We enrolled you in a drawing class," my dad said.

"There's more," Susan said, handing me another gift. I tore off the wrapper. It was a box of watercolor paints and a brush.

"It's real sable hair," my dad said. "Professional artists paint with these brushes."

"It belonged to my father," Susan said. "He used to do a bit of painting, but now his arthritis is too bad."

Susan looked at my dad with big eyes. I could tell she liked him and she was happy to be here. I held the brush and the box of paints in my hand. I was so excited looking at all the colors. I don't know why, but I got up and gave her a hug.

"I love it," I said, putting my arms around her.

When we finished opening presents, I sat by the fire. I was very happy with my gifts, but I secretly wished there would be something under the tree from my mother. I was convinced it was hidden under the other presents, a card even, inviting me to come visit her in the new year. The truth was, there was nothing, not even a card.

I fell asleep while my dad and Susan drank wine and talked by the fire. When I woke, everyone had gone to bed, and the room was dimly lit from glowing coals in the fireplace. I went upstairs to my room.

That night, I dreamed of my mother. We were sitting by a lake, talking. *Things aren't always as they appear to be,* my mom said. My head was on her lap. *Why don't you see me?* I asked. She put her hand in my hair. *No, I can't,* she said. And just as I was about to ask her why, she jumped into the lake and swam away like a mermaid.

I woke in the morning to the sound of dishes clanking. Someone was emptying the dishwasher. I walked downstairs and into the kitchen.

"Good morning, Jeremy." It was Susan, and she was cooking pancakes.

For some reason at that moment I thought of Evan facing a back operation after the holiday. It occurred to me that to him my mother was probably a kind of intruder in his life like the way Susan was in mine.

"Good morning," I said. And Susan smiled.

13. After Christmas, Susan was at our house more nights than she wasn't. Neither Julie nor I had much to say about it, and my dad never explained anything.

A month into the new year, Susan officially moved in her cat, Pippin. I wouldn't have minded so much if the cat had been nice, but it hid behind doors and ambushed my feet as I walked by. The only person it didn't attack was Susan.

Things started changing around the house. The old green curtains were replaced with lighter, white ones. New towels and sheets, even silverware and plates, suddenly appeared. One day a truck arrived, delivering a new bed and bed frame for my dad's bedroom. Uncle John came over with his pickup to help move the old furniture out and bring it to the dump.

In early February I went with Dad to pick up my grandma Amelia and bring her to our house for the weekend. I saw so little of my grandma that I sometimes forgot I had one. I wondered why I hadn't seen her through all of this. I guess maybe it was because she was closer to my mother than she was to her own son.

Grandma Amelia's apartment was on the sixth floor of a brick building in New Rochelle, New York. We took the elevator up, its old chains clanking; the small space smelled like a combination of roasted turkey and mothballs. In the past, the only time I saw my grandmother was when my mom and I went to clean her apartment. Both the apartment and my grandma were messy, so my mom would start sweeping, vacuuming, dusting, cleaning mirrors, and finish by giving Amelia a bath. I helped with the dusting and taking the trash out to the incinerator.

The hallway was painted red, with red carpets. Vases of fake flowers sat on small tables. Dad knocked on the door. "Amelia!" he shouted. I always found it odd that he called his mom by her first name.

"Coming—*espera, espera*," a voice said. We heard at least four locks and latches clicking before the door finally opened.

The floor was covered with piles of magazines.

"Just a minute—*espera*," Grandma said, moving some magazines aside so she could open the door completely.

"Amelia," my dad yelled. "Don't you ever clean this place?" He walked into the kitchen. "Aren't there any clean glasses?" He ran the faucet, and red water gushed and sputtered. "Dirty dishes, no water . . . how does she live here?" My dad pushed aside an open bag of cookies and some paper wrappers from fast-food hamburgers. A cockroach scuttled out of a wrapper and crawled over his arm.

"Jesus Christ," he said, shaking his arm. "Oh, my God." He tried opening a cabinet, but it was stuck closed. He shook his head. "I don't want to know."

My grandma snuck up from behind and pinched me just above the waist. I jumped four feet, thinking of that roach.

"Ouch!" I said, turning around.

"*Joo, joo, joo,*" she said, pinching me again. She couldn't speak English very well. She was born in Brazil and mostly spoke Portuguese with my dad. My sister and I thought she was nuts, but it was hard to tell because we couldn't understand her.

Last time I'd been there with my mom, the place was much cleaner. I didn't need to ask. I could tell my mom had not been around in a while. Taking care of Grandma was always Mom's duty. Dad stayed away.

Dad glanced at the books on the shelf behind the chair where my grandfather, Otakar, used to sit.

"Get your bag and let's go," Dad said, giving her a swat on her bottom.

I sat on my grandmother's couch. From there, through the window, I could see into a park. Squirrels chased one another's tails, while a woman pushed a baby stroller. My eyes focused on the painting of a young woman that hung over the couch.

"That's your grandmother," I could hear my mom's voice say.

"It can't be," I'd said.

"It is. Your grandma was a beautiful woman. When grandfather took her to Europe on their honeymoon, there was a beauty contest on the cruise ship. Guess who won?"

"Grandma?"

My mom had nodded.

I looked at my grandmother across the room, purple half-moons under her eyes, dense and dark like figs.

"Amelia!" my dad yelled again. She stood in front of him with a suitcase and a plastic bag filled with things. I could only imagine what he was saying, because he was speaking in Portuguese. I think he asked why she had so much stuff for just one night.

Grandma Amelia thought it was Christmas, even though Christmas was more than a month gone. She brought us things from Macy's that my sister said were stolen (Grandma had been arrested for shoplifting once). She put blocks of American cheese in our fridge, big enough to build a fort with. My dad took the cheese out and chucked it in the woods.

"This is Amelia," my dad said. "Amelia, this is Susan."

My grandma shook Susan's hand.

When no one was looking, Grandma put a stack of *National Geographic* magazines on the living-room table.

Susan walked into the living room a little while later. She was about to remove the magazines when a cockroach crawled out from between the pages.

"Eeeek . . . Carl!"

I hid my laughter.

"What?" my dad said, racing into the living room.

"Get those magazines out of here!" Susan said. "Grab her purse, all of it, out. They're everywhere! Roaches. There are roach eggs all over everything.

Do you know how hard they are to get rid of?"

My dad listened to her. He brought all of my grandmother's belongings out onto the driveway.

Grandma stood next to him.

"Amelia! Don't you bring us any more presents, understand?" He continued to yell at her in Portuguese.

That night Grandma slept in my room and I slept on a spare mattress in Julie's. Neither Julie or I was happy with the arrangement, but it reminded me of when we were younger and shared a room. She took care of me like one of her dolls. But then Dad finished off the screened-in porch, it became Julie's room, and we never talked as much again.

The walls of Julie's room were painted pink, and above her bed was a collage of magazine cutouts and photos of friends. The room overlooked the backyard and the garden, overgrown with weeds. She had her own bathroom, a big closet, and a phone.

Next to a mirror there was a poster my mom had

bought her, of a man standing in front of a Rolls-Royce, one foot propped up on the bumper. He was dressed in riding boots, tight pants, and a white shirt, and he was holding a pair of white gloves in one hand and a glass of champagne in the other. The poster read, POVERTY SUCKS!

At least once a month my dad asked Julie to take the poster down. "I hate that poster," he said. "It reminds me of your mother."

"It's my room," Julie replied.

"It's my house," my dad said.

But the poster stayed.

"Dad doesn't like that thing, Julie," I said to her now. "You should take it down."

"Whatever, Jeremy," she said, brushing her blond hair in front of the mirror. "It's my room and I can do what I want."

"It's not like we're poor," I said.

"Compared to my friends we are. When Carey's grandmother comes to visit, they go to the city and have tea at the Ritz."

"Yeah, but I bet her grandma doesn't bring roaches in old magazines."

"See what I mean? Our family is crazy."

"Yeah, but we're not poor."

"Dad never buys me anything," Julie said, separating three strands of her hair to make a braid. "I mean, I don't even get an allowance. Mom used to buy all our clothes at thrift shops, remember?"

"I remember she'd change the price tags on things at the supermarket."

"Yeah, see?"

"Yeah."

"I'm not going to be poor," Julie said, turning to look at the progress of her braid in the mirror. "You know, Mom used to steal stuff for me."

"Really?"

"She stole this coat for me once at Macy's. She put it on me and we just walked out the door. Now she can buy anything she wants."

"What do you mean?" I asked.

"I mean, Paul buys her whatever she wants."

I stopped and looked at her. "What? How do you know?"

"She tells me."

"Have you seen her?"

"I see her now and again."

"But where is she? Does she live close by?"

"Yes." Julie took her blond hair together in her hands and tied off her braid with a rubber band. "She asks about you. Sometimes you're all she talks about."

"What do you say?"

"I tell her things you tell me. Things about school, how you're doing in sports, your drawings, whatever. But usually I say, 'Why don't you call him and find out?'"

"And what does she say?"

"'I don't want to upset your father.'"

"I don't think I want to know."

"Jeremy. Please don't tell Dad."

"He doesn't care," I said. "He knows he has no control over you."

"Still." Julie picked up one of her teen magazines.

"But that's so weird."

"What's weird?" she said, flipping the pages.

*That you're seeing our mother and I'm not! That
she asks about me. That I feel left out of some party I
wasn't invited to. That's what's weird!*

"Nothing," I said.

14. *My drawing classes at Silvermine Art School*
began in late February. Every Tuesday and Thursday
afternoon, my dad drove me the twenty minutes from
our house to the school.

The class met in a small studio with white walls.
The students sat in a circle around our instruc-
tor, Jack, who taught us drawing techniques, like
perspective—how to make something look three-
dimensional on a two-dimensional page.

"You create depth," Jack said, "by the use of light
and shadow. Take this orange," he continued, holding
up an orange. "I put it on the table by the window,
and the light coming through casts a shadow beneath
it. It you're working in color, you study to see what
color the shadow is. You think shadows are all the

same color? Look more closely." We gathered around. The orange sat on a white sheet. "Tell me, what colors do you see?"

The students shouted out different things, but the truth was, none of us had thought of a shadow as anything but gray. All of a sudden, looking at the shadow cast on the white sheet, we saw orange, and purple, and yellow.

"Being an artist," Jack said, "isn't just about making pictures. It's a different way of life. You're no longer seeing the world as a normal person—you're observing things, taking them apart, studying them, learning all the time. Making art is what you do all the time. Drawing and thinking about art doesn't stop when you leave this room. If it does, you're not an artist."

In the last half hour of the first class Jack paired each student with a drawing partner. Mine was a cute, small, dark-haired girl with dark eyes named Casey. We pulled up our chairs so that we faced each other, and every five minutes we took turns drawing or being the model. I had trouble drawing her.

I couldn't focus with her looking at me. I pretended she was a bird. But birds rarely look you in the eye.

After class I sat outside and waited for my dad to pick me up. He was late. All the other kids were gone. I watched the seagulls overhead. There was a bigger bird too, mostly white, with broad wings. Compared to the slender gulls this bird looked powerful. I watched it circle. Something about it reminded me of Casey. I studied it. Its path seemed to draw the outline of her face, the curve of her nose, the space between her lips. Then the bird was gone.

I ran behind the school to look for it. Behind the building the Silvermine River flowed by, dark and cold. The water swirled around big boulders. When I turned back, I was facing the back of the school for the first time. It had a row of tall glass windows. The glass reflected the trees, but I could also see into the room.

An adult painting class was taking place. The artists stood at their easels drawing a model, who was completely naked, lying on a couch. The model's long black hair was wrapped around her white shoulders; her legs were covered by a blanket, her toenails painted red.

I ran back to the parking lot where Susan was waiting in her car to take me home.

Before going to bed, I sat at my desk with my sketchbook and pencils, outlining the body of the nude model. It was eleven thirty before I put the drawings away and fell asleep.

Tuesdays and Thursdays became my favorite days. I looked forward to drawing and talking with Casey at the end of every class. One day Casey picked up my sketchbook and started flipping through.

"Wow," she said, calling me over. "These are amazing." She turned the book toward me so I could see my own work.

"Oh, those?" I said. My palms were sweating.

Casey handed me back the sketchbook because it was my turn to draw her. I turned to a new page and began to make marks with a piece of charcoal. She looked away, and I stared at her profile. Her shirt was unbuttoned on top, and the collar was loose around her neck. She had a small bump on her nose. I started drawing her but ended up drawing an owl. She was too pretty to draw.

"My mother's an artist," Casey said, still looking away. "She teaches painting here. She models for adult classes to make extra money."

"Oh," I said.

Her white skin, brown eyes, long black hair.

After class Jack announced that our next class would end an hour early. I put away my things when Casey said, "Don't tell your dad about class ending early. We can spend that hour together."

I was shocked.

"Okay," I said softly.

That night and the next two days I imagined what would happen in the hour alone with her. I imagined we'd sit together, or maybe another kid from class would be there waiting and it would all be ruined, or we might sit by the river and talk.

What would she say? What would I say?

Thursday, class ended at five, and, as planned, my dad would not be there until six. Casey put away her easel and handed me her sketchbook.

"Can I look at your drawings?" I asked. I hoped she remembered the plans we'd made.

"Sure," she said.

I flipped through page after page. All of the pictures were of me. She'd almost filled the entire book.

"Wow," I said. "These are really good. I mean, not just because they're of me."

She took my hand in hers and closed her sketchbook. "They're okay," she said.

My palms were sweaty. I was afraid she'd notice. She wouldn't let go.

"How old are you?" Casey asked, looking at me squarely.

"I'm twelve," I lied. I was three months from turning eleven.

"How old are you?" I asked her.

"I'm thirteen."

My heart pounded loudly under my shirt.

"Jeremy," she said very slowly, letting each syllable come out one at a time, "why don't you come back to my house. I want you to meet my dog. She's a cute little pug named Sugar. We can wait there until your dad comes."

"Okay," I said. "Can we walk to your house?"

"Yeah. It's just down the path by the river."

On the path, we passed the long row of windows where I'd first seen the nude model. Casey led me down along the river until we came to a footbridge. We crossed and walked through a grove of old hemlocks to a small wooden house.

"Oh," Casey said, "my mom's home. Come in and meet her?"

"Okay," I said.

Casey's mom, the model, was standing in the kitchen with a light-colored dress on, barefoot, her toenails painted red. She was reading part of that day's paper.

"I love your braid, Mom," Casey said.

"You would, honey—you made it."

Her voice was soft.

"This is Jeremy, from my class."

"Hi, Jeremy from my class," her mom said, putting down the paper.

A small black dog raced into the kitchen from the hallway.

"Sugar!" Casey shouted, kneeling down to greet her pug. The dog lay on its back with its short little legs in the air, snorting like a pig. Casey turned to me. "Isn't she the cutest dog?" she said, half to me, half to the pet. "Yes, you are. Yes, you are!" The dog got on its feet and ran away.

"Well, nice to meet you, Jeremy," Casey's mom said. "I've heard all about you."

"*Mom,*" Casey said.

"Would you like a freshly baked cookie?" her mom asked, holding a plate in front of me. I put my sketchbook down on the kitchen table and took one.

"Thank you," I said. The chocolate chips were warm.

I saw a hand reach for my sketchbook.

"Mom," Casey said, "look what Jeremy's done."

I couldn't believe it! Her mother was looking at the nude pictures I drew of the woman with long black hair. *Does she recognize herself?*

"Talented boy," the mother said, flipping through the pages. She looked at me. "Do you want a glass of milk?"

"Excuse me?" I asked.

"No, Mom," Casey interrupted, "we're fine."

"Okay, dear," she said. "I'm heading over to the school in a few minutes."

Her mom left the kitchen.

"Let's go," Casey said. "I'll show you around the house."

Casey led me into a large room with high ceilings and big windows.

"This is my mom's studio," she said. "This is where we draw."

A long, flat table stretched nearly around the whole room. On top of the table were paint tubes, paper, canvases, pastels, sticks of charcoal, and pencils.

There were large paintings on the walls of the studio, and the wood floor was spattered with paint. Many of the paintings looked like the river, which you could see outside the big windows, but without trees or rocks or sky.

"She's good, isn't she?" Casey said.

"Yeah," I said. "She's really good."

"Oh," Casey said, looking at a clock on the wall. "It's almost six thirty. You'd better go back to meet your dad."

"Yeah," I said, "I guess I should."

Casey walked me outside. "It's always your dad picking you up, huh?"

"Yeah."

"What about your mom?"

"She left, almost a year ago."

"My dad left when I was eight," Casey said. "Well anyway, see you Thursday."

I walked back to Silvermine with my sketchbook under my arm, feeling dizzy in the cool spring air.

The birds sang loudly. The river was up from some rain we'd had the night before. It started to drizzle, so I put my sketchbook under my shirt.

By late March the ice on the ponds melted. I was happy to fish with Stephen again. I was also happy because I got to see Casey. She was always there, her big brown eyes staring at me, charcoal smeared on her white hands.

I told Stephen about her.

"Has she taken off her clothes for you?" he asked, casting in Grady's Pond.

It was funny Stephen should mention that. I imagined that one day I would go over to Casey's, and she'd pull her dress up over her head and pose for me on the couch in her mother's studio.

15. "I think you're cute," Casey told me one Tuesday after class.

"You are too," I said.

Casey smiled, and I felt a surge of energy go through my body.

"Your dad's late again," she said. "Let's go down by the river."

"Okay." We sat next to each other on the river-bank. I looked at the currents moving over the stones.

"Is your mom seeing anyone?" I asked.

"She has boyfriends coming and going all the time. I mean, look at her, she's beautiful." She paused. "What about your dad?"

"Kind of." I nodded and kept staring.

"I want you to draw me," Casey said.

"Draw you?"

"Yes. Come over Thursday after class and draw me. Tell your dad you're having dinner with us, and I'll tell my mom you're coming over."

On Thursday before my dad dropped me off, I told him I was going to dinner at a classmate's house near the school. He could pick me up at the school at eight thirty.

"Oh," my dad said. "Jeremy, I'm so glad you're making friends. This art school is good for you."

"Thanks, Dad," I said, dismissing his comment. "See you later."

Was I acting like Julie?

All through class I was nervous. I'd never been so nervous. I had to wrap my arms around myself to keep from shaking.

Casey and I drew each other at the end of class without speaking. I focused on one of her eyes, a globe, with rivers and mountains, a whole world in itself. When Jack announced that class was over, we gathered our things and put them in our lockers.

I followed Casey to her locker, hoping she'd remember our plans. What if she forgot to tell her mom I was coming to dinner? What if I'd imagined our whole conversation?

"Ready?" she said.

"Um, yeah," I said.

I didn't want anyone to see us leaving. We were almost running. When we got to her house, Casey reached under the doormat to get the key and let us in.

"Do you want something to drink?" she asked. "We have juice, milk, or water."

"No," I said. "I'm fine, thank you."

"Okay," she said, and grabbed my hand and pulled me into her mother's studio.

"You sit here," she said, pointing to a wooden chair.

"Okay."

She stepped over to the green couch, flipped off

her sandals in one swoop, then looked at me.

"Ready?"

"Yeah."

I reached down to grab some charcoal. Casey pulled off her dress in one motion and sat on the couch in her yellow underwear. It was just as I'd imagined.

"How do I look?" she asked.

"Uh, great," I said. But I was so worried her mother would walk in and see us, I had trouble looking at her. As I moved the charcoal across the paper, it seemed my hands were guiding my eyes, not the other way around.

Against the green couch her skin was like snow, light and freckled. Her nipples were small and pink. She wasn't much different from a boy, but at the same time she was so different. Her legs were thinner. Her long black hair was like the charcoal itself.

We sat silently for a long time. Then Casey said, "I'm cold. Can you hand me that robe over there?"

I got up and walked over to her. I put the robe in front of her, and she grabbed my hand.

I leaned over, and she kissed me on the lips.

She got up, grabbed her dress and sandals, and ran out of the room.

I gathered my things and waited for her in the kitchen. She came in wearing pants and a sweater.

"I think you'd better go," she said. "My mom will be home soon."

"But what about dinner?" I asked.

"I don't feel well." Casey walked me to the door.

I walked back in the dark to the school, thinking about Casey.

Did I do something wrong?

The building was still open, and I went to the pay phone to call my dad. Thankfully he was there and didn't ask any questions.

All weekend I thought about Casey, and then Tuesday at class she wasn't there. I was sick thinking about her until Thursday. I finished my drawing of her in her mother's studio, and I decided I was going to give it to her. I hoped she'd fall in love with me and invite me to her house again.

She didn't look at me all during class on Thursday, and then when it came time to draw each other we didn't speak. After class I followed Casey.

"I've been waiting to give you this," I said. I had the drawing rolled up.

Casey went to the corner of the room and unrolled the drawing.

"I don't look like that," she said.

"But it's only a drawing. Of course it's not you, exactly. You're so pretty."

"I look like a boy."

"Well, you're a girl. You're not like your mom yet."

"What?" she said, and started crying. She threw my drawing at me and left the room.

"Casey!" I said, running after her. But she was gone.

•   •   •

I sat on the bench.

What did I do wrong?

What did I do wrong?

What did I do wrong?

At night I dreamed about her.

Will I ever see her again? Will I ever be able to draw her again? Will I ever have another partner like her?

I woke up from my dreams sweating.

I worried all weekend.

I wrote her a long note. Was I going crazy? I wrote that I hoped I'd be invited for dinner and that we'd get married one day. I wanted to teach her how to fish, to bring her to my camp in the woods.

Against all my instincts I went to Julie's room Monday night, the night before our last drawing class.

I knocked on the door.

"What's up?" Julie asked. She was sitting on her bed with headphones on, listening to music. Some textbooks were scattered around.

"Can I come in?"

"Sure." She made some room on her bed, and I sat down.

"I've got something to ask you."

"What?" she asked, taking off her headphones and putting them around her neck.

"About . . . about . . . um . . ."

"A girl?"

"How did you know?"

Julie shrugged. She filed her nails while I told her the whole story.

"My conclusion is," Julie said, "that it's not all about you."

"What?"

"I know you think the world revolves around you, but it doesn't. It's not about you, Jeremy."

"What do you mean?"

"She likes you. She took off her clothes. Then she felt stupid and asked you to leave."

"But what did I do wrong?"

"Nothing."

"Wow," I said. "Nothing?"

"Who said everything in life was going to make sense? You should know this by now. My advice is . . . give her the letter you wrote. If she's ready to talk to you, she will. If she's not, she won't."

"But when will she be ready?"

"It could be a week—it could be never."

Tuesday was our last class, and Casey wasn't there. I gave the letter to Jack and asked if he could give it to Casey's mom.

16. May came quickly and brought warm air and daffodils. The one year anniversary of my mother leaving had come and gone, and no word from her. At one point I'd even thought of asking Evan about her, but he had disappeared too. After his operation no one heard from him and there were rumors he was going to private school. The bass in the pond were biting, but I wasn't that interested in fishing.

"I warned you about those art chicks," Stephen said when I told him what had happened.

"Yeah," I said. But Casey wasn't the only thing on my mind.

"Just goes to show, women are nothing but trouble. I'm going to be alone, like Uncle Stanley."

• • •

At first, Susan seemed timid and nice. But after a few months of living with us, she started to tell my dad and me how to eat.

"Carl," she said at dinner one night, "tell your son he eats like a wolf. I will not watch Jeremy licking his plate and knife! I don't care what day it is."

That particular night was my eleventh birthday.

But the courage to cause trouble only came after her first drink. As soon as she drained the martini glass, she'd say something or start crying.

"What?" Dad asked.

"Nothing," she said softly. Then, louder, *"Nothing."*

"Well, if it's nothing," he said, "I can't help you."

"It's work, what do you think? My boss works me too hard. She's having an affair with the head of the company. I can't say anything to anyone about it or I'll get fired."

"So quit."

"Carl, you know I can't afford to quit. Julie's seventeen . . . she'll be going to college in the fall."

"We'll make it work," my dad said very quietly.

Susan is going to help my dad pay for Julie's college? How did that happen?

I dipped my finger in the sauce on my plate and stuck it in my mouth. Susan gave me a look like I'd murdered someone.

"Your sauce is too good to let it go to waste," my dad said in quick defense.

"Nice try, Carl. Nice try. *Damn it!*" she screamed. "You're no better. You both eat with your faces in your plates. Can we please have some manners around here? Or am I asking too much?"

Susan took her napkin off her lap and threw it on the floor.

"And didn't anyone teach you two about putting down the toilet seat?" she screamed, getting up from the table.

She left the room.

"She wants the best for you, Jeremy," my dad said. "Try to love her. Treat her well."

"I'll try," I said, "but I can't fake it."

"Maybe you could try eating your food the way Susan wants you to—at least when she's around. For me. Okay?"

"Okay."

My dad got up from the table. "Wait here, Jeremy." He returned in a few minutes with an ice cream cake and eleven lit candles.

"Happy Birthday, my big Jeremy," he said.

I saw tears in his eyes.

I closed my eyes and blew out the candles.

17. *That summer my dad and Susan went on* a three-week trip to New Mexico. I stayed at Uncle John's. My cousin Jill was away at camp so I would be sleeping in her room.

I didn't mind staying at Uncle John's. He had summers off and would take me fishing.

I packed my fishing rod, some lures, and my journal in the duffel bag with my clothes. I stood by my desk deciding whether to bring my drawing materials.

"Come on, Jeremy," my dad said. He was carrying soda bottles and milk jugs full of water to the door. "It's time to head to Uncle John's."

"What are you doing with that water?"

"Uncle John is having water problems."

I grabbed two bottles and helped my dad carry them to the car.

"Dad?" I asked. "Why do you and Susan have to go away for so long?"

He didn't answer.

"You know, Jeremy, Susan wants badly for you to feel as if . . . you know, that she can be like a mother to you."

"But she's not my mother," I said.

"Jeremy, keep your voice down."

"I don't care if she hears me."

"Come on, then," my dad said, putting the last bottle in the trunk, "let's go."

As my dad and I drove up Main Street in Monroe, I remembered what the land had looked like even four years before.

"Dad," I said as we passed a new supermarket, "where did that farm go? Remember when there used to be cows here? And the small cemetery on the hill?"

"Things change, Jeremy. Not always for the better."

I could see now—they had blasted the hillside where the cows used to graze to make a level parking lot for stores. Behind it on a small hill the cemetery was still there.

When we pulled in, Uncle John was working on a car in the garage, its parts scattered on the driveway and the lawn.

Being at my uncle's felt like being in a cabin in the wilderness. It seemed as though we were far from civilization and everything always needed fixing. My dad started to carry the jugs of water from the car to the house.

"Good, you brought the water," Uncle John said.

"What's the matter?"

"The well's going dry. I don't mind, but Janice is going crazy."

When we brought all the water into the kitchen, Uncle John took us out the back door to show us how he'd temporarily hooked up a hose from their pool to the toilet in the house so it would flush.

"See, Carl, I had to hook up the pump to this temporary water tower." The tower was a washbasin on top of some crates. "That way I don't have to pump it all the way."

"Use gravity, save money," my dad said.

Though my uncle was proud of this quick fix, when Aunt Janice stepped out on the back porch, her arms were folded across her chest, and she was shaking her head.

The meeting was awkward. Aunt Janice was ready to yell at Uncle John, but she had to be civil because my dad was there.

"Well," Aunt Janice said, "we're so happy to have Jeremy for three weeks. I know John's been looking forward to it."

My dad looked at his watch. "Oh, I'd better go. We have to catch our plane."

"Have a good time," my uncle said, pulling a rag out of his back pocket and wiping his hands.

Uncle John made a cold bean salad and a jug of sweet iced tea, and we ate under the grape arbor on the porch. After lunch he took my duffel bag up to Jill's room and set it on the bed next to her stuffed animals. I looked out the window.

"I'll be out in the barn," Uncle John said. "Why don't you meet me there when you're settled?"

I laid out my clothes on the bed, along with my rain jacket, my journal, and my pencils. I put my boots in a corner of the room before going out to the barn.

When I got down to the barn, Uncle John was loading things in the truck: a shovel, a pickax.

"Let's take a ride," he said.

We drove down Wheeler Road, not far from the house, and pulled off into a dirt parking area.

"I just bought this property," he said. "See the house down there? I've started fixing it up."

It was a tiny house, like a cabin, in bad need of repair.

"See those stones over there?" There was a big pile of stones in the corner of the property. "You can help me build them up into a wall. Maybe even outline a flower bed."

New England, my dad once told me, had the mixed blessing of being littered with stones. They were left behind when the glaciers melted at the end of the last ice age. In order to grow crops, the settlers who first arrived in the mid-1600s had to move them. Sometimes they just piled them up to get them out of the way, but usually they made walls. The stone walls kept the livestock on their property, and they also looked nice. You could see the walls everywhere, some more than three hundred years old.

My uncle took my arm and told me to make a muscle.

"You're pretty strong, Jeremy" he said. "I guarantee you'll be stronger when we finish this wall."

I looked up at him. He was six foot two and more than two hundred pounds—all muscle. I was eleven and just five feet tall exactly. I couldn't imagine ever being as tall and strong as he was.

He took me around the house and showed me what needed to be fixed.

"See," he said, "all these boards around the foundation are rotten. I'm tearing out the floor, and the roof has to be replaced. The pipes are lead. I need to take them out, bring everything up to code."

"You're doing all this yourself?" I asked.

He nodded. "When it's all done, I'm going to rent it out."

We drove back to the house and sat under the grape arbor. Uncle John lit a cigarette and looked toward the barn. You could see the humidity in the air. Rusty ran up to us and nuzzled her head in her master's lap. There was an elm tree stump in front of us with tall grass growing up around it. In old photos the big tree was still there, my cousins leaning against its trunk while my uncle kneeled next to them holding fish they'd caught. They no longer fished with him, and the tree had died from a disease brought over accidentally on ships from Europe.

Uncle John tapped out his butt in a clam shell he used as an ashtray. Then he lit another cigarette. Just then we heard the garage door close. Aunt Janice had come home from work. She stepped out onto the porch through the creaky red door to the garage. She was dressed in a suit, and she braced her hips with her hands like she was expecting something.

"How was your day?" Aunt Janice asked.

"Good," Uncle John said. "How was yours?"

"Oh, fine." She looked around. "You been just sitting here?"

"No, actually. I was thinking of grilling something for dinner."

"Good," my aunt said. "We have hamburger meat in the freezer."

"You want hamburgers, Jeremy?" my uncle asked.

"I'll eat anything," I said.

My uncle lit the grill. Then we went inside to defrost the hamburger meat and make the patties. When we came back outside I took off my shoes and felt the cool grass and dandelions under my bare feet. It was peaceful, watching the heat waves rise off the grill, the barn swallows catching the last insects of the day.

The stillness was interrupted by Aunt Janice yelling from the second-story bathroom.

"John! The toilet still doesn't work."

"I know," he said, putting the hamburgers on the hot grill. "There's not enough water pressure to use the upstairs bathroom. I told you, you have to use the downstairs one."

Aunt Janice slammed the window shut.

There was silence.

"Why does she do that?" my uncle asked.

He wiped sweat from his brow.

"Watch the burgers, Jeremy. Flip them in a minute."

Uncle John went inside, and I heard some shouting.

"Christ, John, you're here all day doing nothing. I come home from work and all I want is to have a working toilet. It's been two weeks—can't you fix it? Is that too much to ask?"

"I told you, the well isn't deep enough. It's summer. It's dry. If you want to put up the money to drill a deeper well, fine. Otherwise we wait for rain."

After dinner Uncle John and I watched a baseball

game on TV. I fell asleep on the couch. When I woke the TV was off and it was dark outside. I went up to Jill's room to go to sleep. But I couldn't sleep. I missed home. I even missed Julie.

Where in the hell is Julie?

Through the bedroom window I could see the barn, the roof lit up silver by the moon. Behind the barn I could see the field, and at the edge the white pines that marked the back of the property. I saw a figure moving, a person. My uncle. What was he doing out there so late?

I got back in bed and tried to sleep.

In the morning we drove to the cabin on Wheeler Road and started building the stone wall. I carried stones to Uncle John. He either found a place for them or tossed them in a pile.

"See, Jeremy," he said, "every stone has its place. If I don't see it at first, I put it aside." By watching him I started to see patterns in his work. I could see what stone fit and what stone didn't. Eventually, I worked on the wall alone and my uncle went to work on other parts of the house.

I found that, day by day, I could lift larger stones all by myself.

"I think you're getting stronger, Jeremy," my uncle said. I was pleased that he noticed.

I knew it would have been easier if he'd bought an empty piece of land and started from scratch. But I saw the beauty in taking something down to its bare parts, the ground torn up, the roots and rocks exposed.

I watched him. Some of his tools were the same ones that I used. He used a pencil to mark a piece of wood before he sawed, to draw a grid on the plywood so he knew where to drive the nail when he held it against the frame. He sharpened his pencil with his knife and handed it to me.

"A carpenter always has a pencil handy," he said. "Put it like this on your ear, so you have it when you need it." Every minute on the site I had my pencil behind my ear, hoping I'd have the chance to use it.

That afternoon Uncle John worked intently on wiring something inside the house. The tarp that covered the holes in the roof cast a dull, blue light inside.

My uncle didn't need me, so I walked outside and down to the spring to get some water. As I knelt down to drink, taking large mouthfuls of cold water, I smelled the scent of mint in the hot, dry air.

I heard a hollow drumming sound echoing from the woods. I followed the sound, walking slowly and quietly, and saw that it was a big woodpecker with a large red crest. I heard my father again saying it was a pileated woodpecker, the largest species of woodpecker in North America, and the only one with a long beak and a tall red crest on its head. I'd never had such a clear view of one outside of a book.

Trying not to startle it, I looked on the ground for something to draw on, and found a discarded piece of wood, about two feet square. It had some marks my uncle drew on one side and was blank on the other. With the pencil I had tucked behind my ear (it almost seemed too convenient it was there), I drew the bird's yellowish beak, its head and triangular crest, and the long sleek form of its coal-black body. It was chiseling a long, thin hole in the tree. I drew and I drew, forgetting about my uncle, about my father and Susan, about home and school.

When the bird flew away, it glided through the woods with sweeping wing beats and let out a loud screeching chatter, *kuk kuk kuk-kuk*, that got louder the farther away it flew. I was eager to show my drawing to Uncle John.

As I walked toward him, my uncle came out of the house into the light. I showed him what I'd drawn. He took his pack of cigarettes from his shirt pocket.

"That's him," he said, lighting a cigarette.

"Have you seen it?" I asked.

"The day I came to look at this property, I saw the spring. I knelt down and felt how cold the water was." He paused and pointed with the hand holding the cigarette. "And I heard this hammering. Rusty went toward it and pointed. The woodpecker stared her down. Looked like an undertaker in that black jacket," he said.

• • •

Uncle John didn't tell Aunt Janice about the bird, the wall, or the cabin at dinner that night. I almost did, but I didn't feel right about it. We just sat and ate in silence.

"I'm going down to the beach to watch the fireworks," Aunt Janice said.

"Oh," my uncle said, "I forgot it was the Fourth of July."

"We were supposed to go out in the boat and watch them, remember?" Aunt Janice huffed. "You were off somewhere and I didn't know if you were even coming back, so I made other plans."

"Okay," Uncle John said.

After dinner my uncle and I walked outside and sat in the wooden chairs at the edge of the grape arbor.

It wasn't dark yet, but I could see flashes in the sky from lightning. The air was hot and muggy and smelled like ferns. Everything looked a strange yellowish green, as if I were seeing through colored lenses. In the distance I heard thunder rumbling.

"Why don't you get your drawing of the woodpecker and bring it out to the barn," Uncle John said. "I'll meet you there."

I went up to my cousin's room to get my drawing, then walked out to the barn.

The barn was cool and still smelled like a chicken coop from when Uncle John used to keep chickens. He sat me down at his workbench. On the bench was an old tackle box. As he opened the lid, I peered over his large hands. Inside were tubes of paint and several brushes.

"Are those yours?" I asked. "I mean, do you paint?"

"Yes," he said. He stopped momentarily and lit a cigarette. "But I don't paint anymore." He coughed. "I was thinking maybe you could use them."

Just then heavy rain began to pound on the roof of the barn. Cracks of thunder roared from the direction of the house, not too far away. "Why don't you try them on your woodpecker?" he continued, uninterrupted by the storm. "Do you remember the colors?

If not, I can get my bird book and we can look up the woodpecker." He walked away from the bench. "I'll get you something to use as a palette."

He brought me a white plate and filled an old jar with water gushing from a rain spout outside the barn doors. He gave me a rag to wipe my brushes, and I began to paint.

I mixed black with cobalt blue and dabbed it on the woodpecker's wings that I'd sketched on the piece of wood. I painted the bird's tall crest. I stood up from the bench to get some perspective. I was frustrated. The detail in my drawing was covered. The painting looked overworked, and the paint wasn't sitting well on the wood surface. How could I get the feeling of feathers with paint? Feathers are transparent, hollow, and light—they are the reason a bird can fly. My feathers looked like lead. I put down the brush. *Where did my uncle go?* I'd gotten so wrapped up in drawing, I hadn't even noticed he'd left. I went outside to look for him.

The thunderstorm had passed, and a cooler, high-pressure system had pushed out the humid air. In the distance I could still see the flashes of lightning.

Or fireworks.

All the lights in the house were out, but at the other end of the property a warm light glowed through the pines. I walked in the direction of the light, down a path through dense ferns. I saw it was coming from a small shed, like a tree house, with a window on the side. My uncle was seated by the open window, reading a book, a steaming mug of coffee in his hand.

"Hey, Jeremy," he said as I walked toward him. "How's your painting coming?"

"Has this always been here?" I asked, too wrapped up in the strangeness of it to answer him.

"I built it for the girls; they used it as a playhouse. I like the quiet back here."

A gust of wind made a *whishhhhhhh* sound in the needles of the pine trees.

"I think tomorrow we'll get up early and go fishing," he said. "We'll give ourselves a break from working on the wall. What do you think?"

I nodded.

"The tide will be outgoing at first light." He got up from his seat and walked outside. "You feel that?" He asked. "The humid air is gone."

"Yeah," I said.

He reached into a paper bag hidden at his side. He pulled out two bottle rockets. We stuck them in the ground.

"You light one and I'll light the other," he said. He handed me a book of matches. I lit one firework and Uncle John lit the other with his cigarette. They shot up into the air with a *phhhhhffft*, spun in circles, popped, and left trails of sparkling light that lingered somewhere behind my eyes.

"Happy Fourth of July," he said.

For the first time since I'd come to stay with my uncle, I went to bed without any worries. I thought about home and Dad and Julie but I didn't miss them anymore.

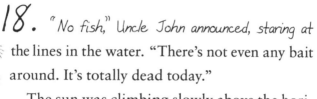

18. "No fish," Uncle John announced, staring at the lines in the water. "There's not even any bait around. It's totally dead today."

The sun was climbing slowly above the horizon, and the air was humid and sticky again. Uncle John pulled the anchor and began reeling in the lines. The river current pulled us under the tall interstate bridge.

"We'll try in the sound," he said. "Maybe troll at Middle Ground."

Uncle John motored slowly out of the channel, until we were out of the no-wake zone. Then he pushed the throttle to full speed, taking us across the open water to a barely visible lighthouse.

The lighthouse stood at the midpoint of Long Island Sound, between Connecticut and the shore of Long Island. It took about twenty minutes to get there from the mouth of the river where we launched the boat. There weren't any waves so the ride was smooth. We dropped the anchor near the giant rocks around the bottom of the lighthouse. A low foghorn sounded.

Ooooooonnnn.

It was a desolate spot, except for a few seagulls perched on the rocks.

Uncle John set the lines with frozen bait since we hadn't caught any live bait that morning. He cast two lines in the current that was forming alongside the lighthouse as the tide changed. All we caught were spider crabs.

They looked like barnacled sea monsters. I didn't mind seeing one on the bait when I reeled in a line, even though they were kind of ugly. *Better than nothing.*

But Uncle John wanted to catch bluefish, maybe even a striper for dinner. He reeled in the lines.

"Let's see if we can change our luck," he said.

He pulled the anchor and turned around to start the engine. The current was pulling us close to the breakwater by the lighthouse. He yanked the pull cord to start the engine, and it snapped.

"Christ!" he yelled.

He slammed his fist down on the wooden seat, and it happened to hit a rusty bait hook. Luckily, the barb didn't go into his skin, but the point did, and his hand was bleeding.

"You all right?" I asked quietly.

"One of those days," he said.

He took the cover off the engine and looked at it for a while. The current pulled us beyond the lighthouse, and now we were far beyond it, just floating in the haze. Uncle John searched for a cord to wrap around the top of the engine. He grabbed a sweatshirt he'd brought and pulled the drawstring from the hood. He wrapped the cord around the engine, and with one hand flat to hold it in place he pulled with the other. The engine grumbled.

"Ha!" he exclaimed. "That's promising."

He wrapped the cord around again and pulled. The engine started.

Uncle John put the boat in gear, and we motored along over the flat water. I watched the hazy clouds reflected in our wake. My uncle was quiet for some time.

"That's the difference between your father and me," he said finally. "Your father would have bought a new engine by now. 'John,' he says, 'what happens if you break down?' Well, you see what happens— you use your head." Uncle John pulled a pack of cigarettes from his shirt pocket and tapped out the last one. He lit it. "My girls are the same. If it breaks, they want a new one. They didn't get that from me."

We motored toward Penfield Lighthouse, a mysterious tower shape standing in the haze. A red light flashed every few seconds as we approached the breakwater. I watched my uncle set an umbrella rig on each line. Six stiff wires tied to each other at one end formed the umbrella structure for the rig. The loose ends of each wire had a hook on them with rubber tubes in different colors to attract the fish. When the rods were rigged he let the lines out as the boat was moving, and set the rods in rod holders in the stern.

I watched the lines cutting through the water as the boat moved, and I listened to the hum of the engine. I thought about our stone wall. I thought about what my uncle said. *It's too easy to give up.* You had to work for things in life, and that made life worth living.

"What's that over there?" my uncle said, turning the wheel.

He grabbed his handheld radio. We headed for the object he saw floating in the water. It was only a plastic bag, partly filled with air, partly underwater.

We continued on, but a heavy fog set in. You couldn't tell land from sky or see either shore. A horn sounded from the lighthouse, a low, eerie *oooooooonnn.*

I knew that a year ago, my uncle had found a dead

body floating in the sound when he was out fishing alone. I figured that that was what was bothering him: He had to check out that plastic bag, to make sure it was just a plastic bag. I had never asked him about it before.

Ooooooonnnn.

I wanted to ask, *Is it true you found a dead body out here?* But the question stayed in my head.

Oooooooooonnnn.

We didn't catch any fish that day. Not so much as a nibble.

19. My uncle and I fished most mornings and in the afternoons I helped him build the stone wall. We finally got some rain and Aunt Janice was happier to have water. Then before I knew it the three weeks were up and my dad came to pick me up at Uncle John's. He didn't look or sound or smell familiar.

"How was it, Jeremy?" he asked as we drove home.

"Fine," I said.

"Did you have a good time with Uncle John? What did you do?"

"We built a stone wall."

"John told me over the phone. That's great." But my dad didn't sound like he was paying attention.

I shrugged my shoulders.

. . .

Susan was in the kitchen preparing lunch when we got back. I remembered what it was like to be in the kitchen in summer. It smelled more like summer there than anywhere. I looked in the fridge for some iced tea.

"Hey, Jeremy," Susan said.

"Hey."

"How was it?"

"I had a good time," I said, and went straight to my room with a glass of tea.

I dropped my bag on the bed and sat down at my desk with the paints Uncle John had given me. I began to draw the pileated woodpecker on a new piece of paper. As I drew, the whole scene came back into my mind. In the bird's feathers I could hear my uncle working in the house, feel the cool air from the spring. I set up my palette and filled a glass with water.

This time I wasn't going to let my picture turn into a muddy mess. I added some red to the top of the woodpecker's head, but not too much, and some blue and black to the wings. I kept the paint thin, and when it dried I added another layer to places where I wanted more color. In this way I made the woodpecker look three-dimensional.

"Light and shadow," I could hear Jack say. "Without shadow, there's no depth."

I was thinking about all the things I'd learned from my uncle, when my dad interrupted, calling me to lunch.

We sat at the kitchen table and ate turkey sandwiches and cucumber salad and a cantaloupe cut in wedges. When my plate was cleared, my dad looked at me and smiled.

He took Susan's hand in his.

"There's something we want to tell you," my dad said.

He turned Susan's hand so I could see a diamond ring sparkling on her ring finger. I had probably known, somewhere deep in my mind, but I hadn't wanted to know, so I'd never really considered what it would be like when it happened. He caught me by surprise.

"We—," my dad began to say.

"No!" I shouted. "No, no, no!"

Before anyone could say anything else, I ran up to my bedroom and locked the door.

"Jeremy," my dad said through the closed door. "It's the best thing for us. Susan and I love each other. One day you'll understand."

I remained quiet. Then, unexpectedly, I heard Susan's voice.

"Jeremy, please let me in. I want to apologize."

I opened the door, but I stayed quiet. I sat on my bed and she sat down next to me.

"I'm marrying . . . married your father because I love him," she said stumbling over her words. "I know you think you love him more. I know I'm not your mom, but I want us to be a family."

I was just hoping she'd stop talking.

"I'm sorry," I said. "I just . . . I don't know."

Susan gave me a hug. Her soft hands on my shoulders didn't feel natural. I sat with my arms at my sides.

"Please, Jeremy, don't be angry at me."

"I'm not angry," I said.

I was so angry.

I waited until Susan left the room. Then I put some things in my backpack, walked past my dad doing dishes in the kitchen, grabbed my fishing rod, and left without saying good-bye.

I walked down the street to the dirt road and up to the reservoir.

I walked and fished my way up the shore, past five familiar coves, and then came to one I didn't know. It was the farthest I'd ever been.

I'll keep going, walk around the reservoir to Stephen's house.

I figured it was about five miles.

I continued up the road through the woods, under the tall maples and oaks. I knew I was being unfair to my dad and Susan. I didn't hate Susan. I just felt like I was being pushed out.

There were places on the reservoir between my house and Stephen's where I'd never fished. I'd always wanted to go to these places. I'd imagined what they were like. I could go there now. Maybe no one had ever fished these coves before.

Think of all the big bass that have never seen a lure.

I kept walking, using my fishing rod to clear cobwebs in my path, thinking I was close to the north end of the reservoir. But there was always a next cove, or a small island blocking the view. After about an hour, I thought I saw it, the place where the Mill River tumbled down a steep ledge into the reservoir. It looked like a white line strung between mountain laurel and hemlocks. Then I could hear it. A waterfall.

I'd caught a few small bass on my way, but now I was too excited to fish. I wanted to reach the top of the reservoir.

I stumbled over boulders and tripped on tree roots and wild grape vines, catching my line on branches and almost breaking my rod. I had to get there. I had to see the river where it entered the reservoir. There was something meaningful in seeing the river, alone, by itself, as it was before they built the dam and flooded the valley, when it was just a wooded gorge filled with brook trout, and Indians hunted grouse and wild turkeys and deer with snares, arrows, and spears. A paradise.

I ran.

I imagined I was an Indian, that my jeans were deerskin and my sneakers moccasins, that my fishing rod was my bow and my backpack my quiver of arrows. I took off my shirt and continued to run, faster and faster through the woods. I ran and ran, and the faster I ran, the sharper everything looked to me: the leaves, the cobwebs, the bark on the trees, the stones, the lichen on the stones. Everything in front of me, behind me, above me, was in focus, and though my feet were touching the ground I felt like I was flying.

Then my toe caught something, kept me from going on, as if someone had cut my wings, and I hit the ground. I let go of my fishing rod and my two palms and wrists came down, scraping the skin off on roots and twigs and stones.

I lay on the ground, folded my arms and rolled in the leaves. My hands were burning and sticky with blood. I looked up at the sky, my head on the tree roots, and when I stopped rolling I could hear the falls.

Luckily my sneaker had come off my foot; it had caught on a low string of barbed wire. I went back to get it and saw the wire, put up by some farmer back when all this land was cleared and fences were strung on cedar posts to keep cows and horses in. The trees around me were tall, sixty years old at least, and they grew around the wire where it was in the way. I took a deep breath, thinking about time passing.

Slow down.

When I reached the falls, I sat on a rock and washed the dirt and blood off my hands. I had bruises on my chest and knees, and my elbow was throbbing. But the cold water made me feel better. I didn't even take a cast. I just watched the tumbling water for a while.

I sat longer and smelled the air, the cool air from the falls mixed with the warm summer air. This was all I needed.

I continued walking, and when I got to a street on the other side with cars and houses, I made my way up the road to Stephen's house. Natalie answered the door.

"Jeremy," she said, "come in."

She sat me down in the kitchen.

"Stephen's out with Stanley. Where have you been? What happened to your hands, your forehead? You're a mess."

"It's nothing," I said. "It doesn't hurt."

"Are you hungry?"

I nodded.

"Hold on, honey—I'll get you something."

She came back to the table with a plate of oatmeal cookies.

"Thanks."

"You know, Jeremy, you're welcome in this house any time. But you've got to tell your father you're here. He suspected you might show up. We worry about you." Natalie breathed in deeply and exhaled. "I'll get the phone."

"Can *you* call him?" I asked. She looked at me and tightened her lips. "Let's wait a minute, can we?"

She nodded.

"Your dad's been through a lot," Natalie said. "Susan's important to him. She's helped him out of it."

"I didn't mean to get angry."

"No, Jeremy. I didn't mean that." She took my hand. "It's okay to be angry."

"Is it?"

"I could never imagine leaving my child the way your mom did. It's not natural. It's not human. You have every right . . ." She had tears in her eyes. "Your mom is sick. You know that, right?"

"Sick?"

"Yes," she said. "She's not a whole person. She has problems, Jeremy. Big problems."

I half smiled. "What kind of problems?"

"She's not stable. For one thing, she drinks too much. She blames her problems on other people. She almost killed your father. She's irresponsible. She never stopped being a child. What's it been, over a year and not a word from her? Not even a letter? God knows, I'm angry. Who could do that?"

She let go of my hand.

"I'm going to call your dad now."

I was surprised when Julie's red Beetle pulled up. I had been expecting my dad. As I said good-bye to Natalie, she gave me a hug.

"Where have you been the last three weeks?" I asked Julie, dropping my backpack and fishing rod in the backseat of her car.

"Chill, Jeremy," she said. "Just get in." She pulled the car out of the driveway.

"Chill? You disappear, Dad and Susan run away to get married, I'm dumped at Uncle John's . . ."

"I thought you liked Uncle John."

"I do. But I wouldn't mind having a choice. It's my summer too."

"You weren't dumped. And besides, Uncle John loves you."

"Where were you?"

"I was at Mom's."

"You were *where?*" I asked.

"I stayed at Mom's for a week; then I went to Carey's."

"What? I don't get it. Did you even know that Dad and Susan were getting married?"

"Yes."

"That's it," I said, grabbing the handle of the car door, "I'm getting out."

"Getting out of what?" Julie said, pulling over, the car tires making ruts in the dirt as she put on the brakes.

"What do you think you're doing?" Julie said. "I'm

bringing you home. Dad's worried sick about you."

"Worried? If he's so worried why didn't he have the nerve to tell me they were getting married?"

"Probably because he was afraid you'd act like this," Julie said. She took out a pack of cigarettes. "You can't expect him to always cater to you." She pulled a cigarette out and lit it, blowing smoke out the open window. "I'm not happy about them getting married either, but you know what? He and Mom are never getting back together. Mom's got someone else, so why shouldn't Dad? I know you had run of the house for a year, and you got used to it, but there's someone else in Dad's life now, and you're going to have to learn to share." Julie put the car in gear and we started home again. "By the way," she added, "do you know what day it is?"

"No."

"Take a guess."

"I don't know."

"It's August thirteenth. I'm eighteen years old."

"I totally forgot, Julie! I'm so sorry. Happy birthday."

"But do you see what I mean? You're not the only one who feels forgotten. Everyone's got their own life. Mom kicked me out of her place after a week because Paul came home from a business trip. She didn't even remember my birthday, and she gave birth to me! I don't expect anyone to notice anymore. No presents, no cake, nothing, but I'm fine with it. In some countries your eighteenth birthday is like the biggest day of your life." Julie threw the cigarette butt out the window. She took out another one and lit it. "I applied to colleges this winter—you think anyone helped me? I don't think Dad even knows how old I am. He's got his own stuff to deal with. But I got in, and I'm just glad I'm getting the hell out of here."

"When are you leaving?"

"In September."

"*This* September? Are you kidding?"

"You'll be fine, Jeremy. You can come visit me this fall. I won't be too far, just Rhode Island. I'm excited to go away."

"But Dad's married, you're going away, Mom pretends I don't exist . . . I'm completely alone!"

"You've been building yourself, I can see it—not just from moving rocks with Uncle John. Your face, your voice. You've grown a lot." Julie touched me on the head. "You're going to be okay. I promise."

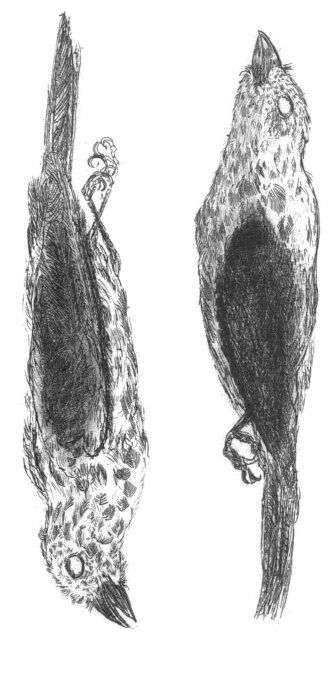

20. *That September, I started sixth grade.* It was my first year of middle school.

"How was your summer?" one of the teachers asked when we sat down for homeroom.

"Do you really want to know?" I said. All the kids laughed, and the teacher gave me a look.

"They never really want to know," Stephen said to me after school as we rode the bus to his house. "They just ask so they can tell us about theirs."

Susan continued to change stuff in our house—the books, the towels, the appliances, the wallpaper—but she still wasn't happy.

"I've been living here for months, Carl, and I

still feel like I'm living in Phoebe's house."

Eventually, my dad let her change almost everything. Susan hired someone to pull out the carpets and finish the hardwood floors underneath them. She put a quilt over the couch and covered the old water-stained wallpaper in the hallway with white paint. She bought a new toaster and new pots for cooking. She wanted to throw out all the living room furniture and start from scratch, but my dad put his foot down.

"I like the furniture. It's perfectly fine," he insisted. "Why spend money needlessly?"

"You don't have to spend the money," Susan said. "I'll buy it on my own."

"I don't want you to buy anymore new furniture. *This is my house*—I like it the way it is. Don't rock the boat! You're lucky I've let you make the changes you have. That's it. Don't bring it up again."

Julie packed two big duffel bags for college. Tension grew between Susan and me over who would claim her room. The day my dad and Susan drove with a carload of Julie's stuff to Rhode Island, I unfolded a card table by the picture window and spread out my paints and paper. I worked there all day and late into the night.

When Susan got home, she complained.

"Dead birds, books, papers—it's a mess in there. You can't even reach the bathroom without tripping over something."

"He's an artist," my dad said from his reading chair. "He needs space."

"Oh, an *artist*," she said sarcastically. "What about me? I'd like a place to set up my sewing machine. I have hobbies too. If I had a space, maybe I'd make something for you."

She stormed upstairs to their bedroom.

Susan kept her sewing things in the closet of Julie's bedroom. Every time she came in to get them she made a comment under her breath.

"It's not my house! It will never be my house," she'd mumble.

I ignored her.

"You know, Susan loves you," my dad said when we were alone.

"Yes, Dad, I know."

"She wants the best for you."

"Yeah, Dad, sure."

"I want you to show her that you love her too. Be good to her. Do it for me."

"I am good to her," I said. "If she had her own kids, she'd realize what an angel I am. I mean what if she had Stephen as a stepson? Then she'd know real torture."

My dad and Susan were about to go for a walk one day, when Susan realized her gloves were missing.

"Where are my gloves?" she asked my dad. "I know I left them in the coat closet. I always leave them on the top shelf. Jeremy must have taken them."

I was sitting at my desk, drawing a kingfisher, a bluish bird that lived on the pond and captured fish with its long beak, when I heard her accuse me. The house wasn't big enough to say anything without me hearing.

"I did not take your gloves!" I yelled from my room.

"Nothing's ever your fault," Susan said.

"I did not take your gloves!" I repeated, going to the top of the stairs.

"Yes, you did!" Susan yelled up the stairs at me. "You think you can get away with anything. Carl, your son is spoiled."

My dad joined Susan at the bottom of the stairs looking up at me. I couldn't tell what he was going to do.

"But I haven't done anything!" I yelled.

"See," Susan said. "I can't win."

I let out a laugh that wasn't meant to be a laugh. The whole thing seemed ridiculous.

My dad's eyes changed. I recognized the look as soon as I saw it. I had forgotten it existed, because I hadn't seen it since my mom left—when I was younger, in another time that felt like another life.

"Come here this minute and apologize to Susan," my dad yelled.

"No," I said. "I won't. You know I didn't do it."

"You're going to apologize," he said, running up the stairs and grabbing my arm. He pulled me down the stairs into the hallway. I pushed him away. He turned around and took my arm again, harder this time, and pulled me into the kitchen.

"Let go!" I said, crying. "I didn't do anything. Why are you taking her side?"

He stood me in front of Susan.

"Carl," Susan shouted, "stop it! Are you crazy?"

"Shut up," my dad yelled to her.

"I didn't mean for you to hurt him," Susan continued. "You're going too far with this. It's just gloves. Now he's going to hate me."

"Say it, Jeremy," my dad said shaking me. "Say, 'It's my fault.'"

I was silent.

"Forget about it, Carl," Susan said. "It's not that big a deal."

"He's going to say it," my dad said, "and you're going to shut up once and for all about your goddamn gloves."

"No!" Susan said. "You're turning it against me."

"Say it, Jeremy. Say it," my dad said. "'*Mea maxima culpa!*'"

Which means, "it's my fault" in Latin. That's the way his father made him say it when he did something wrong. I remained silent and turned my face away from them.

"Say it!" my father screamed, grabbing my hair and turning my head toward her.

"*Mmm . . . ma . . . muma,*" I mumbled intentionally.

"Say it!" he yelled.

"*Mea maxima culpa!*" I said, mocking him, and stuck out my tongue. I broke free and ran upstairs.

"Carl, you're sick," Susan said, taking off her coat and running up the stairs after me. "All this so you can puff your feathers and show me you've done something. Well, you haven't proved anything to me."

"Shut up," my dad screamed. "Shut . . . up!"

He ran up the stairs and grabbed her arm now, pulling her back down.

"Put on your coat. We're going for a walk, and that's the end of it. You can wear my gloves."

"And we'll pretend that everything's normal," she said, crying.

"Yes, we will," my dad said.

As it turns out, Susan's gloves were hidden in a pocket of her coat. She found them on the walk. The next morning, I was drawing in Julie's room, when my dad came in to apologize.

"I don't like getting angry," he said, sitting on Julie's bed near my drawing table.

"I know, Dad," I said, putting down my pencil.

"I have to show Susan we're trying to welcome her."

"Sure, I understand."

"It's just, Susan never had any kids of her own."

"That's my fault," I said, making a joke.

"Well . . . ," he said in a strange tone.

"Are you serious? You're saying it's my fault that Susan doesn't have a kid? What *isn't* my fault?"

"I told her I don't want another child. We agreed to that when we got married, but . . ."

"But what? Now you're thinking of having a kid with her?"

"No, no. We agreed, I told you. No more kids."

"If you have another kid," I said, "I'll run away and never come back. Never, ever. Do you hear me?"

"Don't say that, Jeremy."

"You watch."

I missed Uncle John. I wanted to see him. I missed working with him, missed watching him under the grape arbor in his wooden chair, his feet propped up, my aunt complaining about the water pressure. I wanted to be there with him, and if I couldn't, then I wanted to call him on the phone to hear his voice. But I never called him. I thought it might be weird to just pick up the phone and dial his number. I knew his number by heart. But I couldn't dial it.

It wasn't until early November that I saw him. My dad and I drove over on a Saturday morning to visit. When he stepped out from the cold garage, he reminded me of a caveman. He was slightly hunched over, squinting his eyes in the light, wearing a red plaid wool shirt and jean overalls. He wiped his hands on a greasy rag.

We walked through the door in the garage that led to the kitchen and sat down for breakfast.

"Hey, Carl, what do you say we go hunting?"

"Well," my dad said, pushing a piece of pancake around on his plate, "Susan's with her sister all day. I don't see why not."

"That's great," my uncle said, "'cause Jan's not around either, and Jeremy likes to hunt."

I smiled.

He poured an extra cup of coffee and slipped it in front of me. He pointed to the sugar and winked. I heaved spoonfuls in and stirred the deep-brown drink.

Uncle John took his two shotguns off their racks on the wall in the TV room. He put them on the kitchen counter and dusted the barrels with a rag. Rusty paced back and forth, her claws clicking on the hard linoleum floor.

"She's a great dog," my dad said, scratching her behind the ears.

"Old Rusty, yeah."

My uncle, my dad, and I got in the black truck and headed to Jones's Farm.

We walked up and down the open pastures and through the overgrown fields. It wasn't long before Rusty flushed a grouse, but no one took a shot. The bird was too fast for my dad. Nothing was too fast for Uncle John.

"Why didn't you shoot?" my dad asked.

"There'll be more," Uncle John said.

Minutes later Rusty focused on a patch of brambles. She held a point and my uncle moved in.

"You on something, Rusty?" he asked gently.

"Something's in there," my dad said, raising his gun.

A grouse took off from the ground like an explosion.

Phoosh.

My dad swung his gun and took a shot—*POW*. Then he took another. In one fluid motion, my uncle lifted his gun, swung it toward the bird, and took one shot. It cartwheeled to the ground. Rusty ran up to the grouse and grabbed it in her soft mouth, bringing it to my uncle's hand.

"Thanks, dog," he said.

We stopped in a clearing at midday, and my uncle sat on a stump next to his dog. He was telling my father that he'd quit smoking because of a pain in his chest. My dad said he should see a doctor, but Uncle John said he didn't like doctors. I looked up at the blue, blue sky and saw a few hawks migrating by, high, high up.

It was late for migrating hawks.

21. Winter moved in slowly and stayed late. The snow lingered through the first week of April, but finally spring came, so quickly that I could barely remember there had been a winter at all. After the first few warm days, the buds on the trees exploded, the insect life buzzed, and swarms of birds migrated through our yard.

"A magnolia warbler," my dad said, passing me the binoculars on one of our walks. It was a bird dancing from branch to branch, catching insects in midair. It had a black mask over its eyes and a yellow breast with black streaks.

"Wow," my father said excitedly, pointing to another bird, "what's that? Let me have the binoculars back." He lifted them to his eyes. "See that,

Jeremy?" he said after he'd had a brief look. "That's an indigo bunting." He quickly handed back the binoculars. "Look at the bird first, then keep your eyes on it as you lift the binoculars to your eyes."

There on a wild rosebush was one of the most amazing birds I'd ever seen, so brilliantly blue, it looked as if a light bulb glowed inside its chest. But there was no time to pay attention to the bunting alone. Every few seconds, a new and colorful bird flew in front of our eyes.

"It's a warbler wave," my dad said.

That's how he described this phenomenon, a "wave" of birds. "These birds are coming from Central and South America." He paused to look up at the highest branches of the tree we stood under. "I've always wondered how a small bird could travel such long distances. When I was a sailor, we used to get migrating birds that blew off the shore in a storm— they'd land on our ship to rest. They were so tired, you could walk right up to them and pick them up. They wouldn't move."

I got home early from school one warm spring day and sat at my drawing table by the picture window in Julie's room, thinking of what I was going to make a picture of. Just then, I was startled by the sound of something hitting the window.

Knokkkk.

A bird had flown into the picture window right in front of me. I saw the ghostly shape of the bird on the glass, like an oily fingerprint. I ran outside to see if the bird was hurt, and saw a bright yellow warbler lying on the leaves near my feet. I looked at the window, on the opposite side of the glass from my drawing table. The bird had been tricked by the reflection of the trees and sky in the window. I picked up the bird in my hand and brought it inside. Its body was still warm.

I immediately wanted to make a drawing of it. I took my pencil and started to sketch it out on my paper. It lay there as if it had fallen asleep, its wings spread, its neck in an awkward position. I looked more closely as I made marks on the paper with my pencil. I felt calm, but my breathing made the small downy feathers flutter. I went to put my hand on the bird to turn it over so I could draw the other side, but as soon as I touched it, it came back to life. Suddenly there was a bird flying around my sister's room.

It had only been stunned.

I trapped the bird in the corner of the room and got my hands around it so it couldn't move its wings.

"It's okay, okay," I said to it. "I'm glad you're alive. Don't bite me—I'm just trying to get you to the door to let you out. Don't be scared."

As if talking to it would help.

I walked to the back door with the yellow bird. I pushed the door open with my shoulder, and when I got outside, I opened my hands. The warbler sat in my palm for a second, turned its head to look at me with its black eyes, then flew away.

I heard the phone ringing in the house. I ran inside to get it.

"Hello?" I said, out of breath.

"Jeremy, where's Dad?" I heard Julie's voice, frantic, strained, but I was too excited to notice.

"Julie? Guess what. A beautiful bird—a warbler—just flew into the window, and then—"

"Where's Dad?" Julie interrupted, yelling this time.

"He's at school," I said. "He's at a teacher conference. What's wrong? Are you crying?"

"He's not at school, Jeremy." Her breathing came in sobs.

"Why are you crying? What's wrong?"

"It's Uncle John. He's dead."

"What? What are you talking about?"

"We need to find Dad."

My uncle had been in the gymnasium at school, demonstrating a field hockey drill to other teachers during staff development day. He was running with a field hockey stick across the gym, something he did with his students every day. Suddenly, my uncle was out of breath. His heart seized up, like an engine that stalled unexpectedly, and he dropped to the floor. The other teachers tried to give him CPR, but he didn't respond. He died immediately.

The superintendent could not find my dad, who taught science and astronomy at the same school, or get a hold of my aunt, or Susan, so he called the next number on my dad's emergency list: Julie's number at college in Rhode Island.

"We shouldn't even know this, Jeremy," Julie continued. "Our poor cousins, and Aunt Janice, and Daddy. They don't even know."

My dad had been taking a walk with some other teachers at the edge of the playing fields. He found out soon after we did.

When my father came home later that day, he was in shock. He sat down at the kitchen table and shook his head, saying, "My baby brother's dead." He closed his eyes. "It's impossible. He was only forty-two years old. How could this happen? It seems like yesterday we were children, running around barefoot in the streets, picking lemons in our neighbors' yard. Trapping birds, the most colorful little birds, for the cage on the verandah. My baby brother's dead."

He sounded as if he were trying to convince himself it was true. I couldn't believe it either.

I could hear Uncle John's voice. I could feel the warmth of his flannel shirt on my cheek when I hugged him. I could see his skin, dark from the summer sun, and his dark eyes.

The morning of my uncle's funeral, I dressed in my navy-blue blazer. It didn't fit very well anymore, because my shoulders and arms were bigger. I just started crying, there by my bedroom closet, because my memory of him was still so alive.

The funeral home was not far from our house, but I had never noticed the building before. Uncle John lay in his casket, the top open, in a room with pink curtains. People murmured about a problem with his heart. I wondered why we couldn't just take his heart apart, put it back together, and jump-start it.

My cousins were by the casket in tidy black

dresses. I hesitated next to Julie and Grandma Amelia before I approached the casket. I did not realize how much I was sobbing until I saw my tears fall on his face. I touched his cheek. His skin was cold and hard. I felt selfish for crying.

At the cemetery, my aunt and cousins seemed to levitate, their shiny black shoes hardly touching the dark soil, which was rich like coffee grounds. Before the first handful of earth was thrown down on the box, my aunt asked me to kneel at the edge and lower my uncle's favorite fishing rod on top of his casket. I held the rod, the handle still covered with fish scales, the line through the guides, a swivel tied at the end. I wondered if Uncle John was really in there.

That afternoon I took a walk with my father in the back woods, to a spot where the forest opened up and the land dropped into a hollow. From the top of the hill you could see into the canopy of the trees. Every year at this time we sat there on the trunk of a downed maple tree and watched the bright scarlet tanagers that gathered in the treetops.

"They're here," my dad said, reassured that he'd spotted them.

He once told me they were tropical birds, that their bright colors were misplaced in the northern woods. At the time he compared himself with the birds, a boy from Brazil, now in New England. This time I felt he was talking about his brother.

"Why don't you look, Jeremy," he said, handing me his binoculars.

I'd seen tanagers before, but it always surprised me how brilliant they were. The male birds were red with coal-black wings, and the females were olive-yellow. They were quick and hard to see.

He stood up and backed away from the spot. He sat on a stone wall and put his head in his hands. I went up to him, but he waved me away when he heard my footsteps on the dried leaves.

"Just a moment, Jeremy," he whispered. "Will you give me a moment?"

"It's all right, Dad," I said.

"I know, I know," he said, waving me away with his hand.

He dug his heels through the leaves, into the soil.

"I always thought it was harder for John," my dad said, wiping his tears from his face with the sleeve of his shirt. "I was twelve—it didn't matter as much to me. I had my books. He was only ten. He didn't want to leave. He missed his friends. I wonder sometimes how life would be different if my father had never moved us to this country."

A loud warbling sound came from behind us, in front of us, all around us. It was like the sound a wood thrush makes, but also like a sound we both knew very well.

Whew—whe, whew.

A chill ran up my back to my neck. I thought about the night I had spent at my camp. It wasn't very far from where we were sitting.

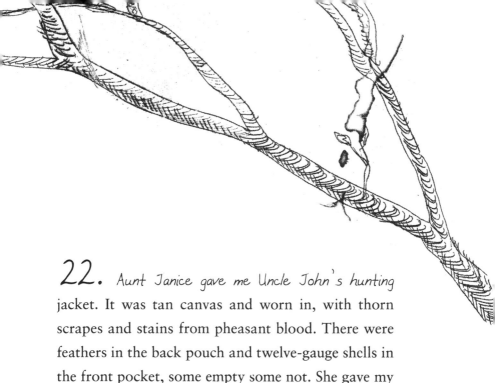

22. Aunt Janice gave me Uncle John's hunting
jacket. It was tan canvas and worn in, with thorn
scrapes and stains from pheasant blood. There were
feathers in the back pouch and twelve-gauge shells in
the front pocket, some empty some not. She gave my
father his lawnmower.

He'd wanted more than anything to have a son,
my mom had once said of my uncle. "So watch over
me," I said out loud to him, looking up at the sky. *I'm
your son too.*

When the weather changed from summer to fall, I
tried on my uncle's hunting jacket for the first time.
The zipper was broken, but my uncle had sewn on
buttons. They were uneven, so when it rained the

water seeped in. The jacket was too big on me—more like a trench coat—but I didn't care.

I'm only twelve. I'll grow into it.

I wore it like a shield at school. No one could bother me as long as I had it on. And no one ridiculed me for wearing it. I wore it on the day my father, Susan, and I went hiking at the Audubon Bird Sanctuary.

Susan didn't know we used to come here with my mother on clear blue days in the fall, to walk up to the top of Godfrey Hill, lie in the field among the low cedars, and watch migrating hawks.

"Let's go to Dirty Swamp Pond," I said.

"We should, Jeremy," my dad said.

"Remember when we saw the heron stab the sunfish and swallow it whole? Head first!"

My father smiled.

We walked together quickly, and soon we were far enough ahead of Susan that we couldn't see her on the path behind us. Suddenly my dad stopped, by a large boulder which was taller than both of us together.

"Let's wait," he said. He took out his handkerchief and wiped his nose. "Do you remember this place? We used to sit here with your mother." He looked up into the branches. Yellow leaves were falling. "She almost destroyed me," he said, not looking at me or even necessarily talking to me. It was quiet enough that you could hear the falling leaves hitting the ground. "I loved her so much," he said. "God knows, I still do."

I nodded.

Susan walked up, and my dad snapped out of his trance. But I couldn't get it out of my head that my father had spoken about my mother that way. She existed on these beautiful days, when, if you looked in the wake of a mallard duck crossing the pond, you could see her reflection. There was a time when she had been happy with us, with our family, and that time was still there, on the surface of Dirty Swamp Pond.

Susan had an allergic reaction to the ragweed flowers that grew at the field edges. She sniffled her way along the paths. Her eyes were red. She was uncomfortable, but she didn't complain. My dad showed her the difference between the bark of a white ash, and that of a sugar maple, or tupelo, or ironwood. She was interested. She caught on fast.

The hawks were high, catching the warm currents of air and riding the southward winds. Winter was coming. Susan looked at them, one by one, as they passed the field where we sat. My father called out the hawks' names as they passed. Other animals were migrating too: monarch butterflies, hummingbirds, swallows. Susan pulled her thick red hair behind her ears. Her fair skin was reddened by the sun. My father took her hand.

I lay down in the field and looked up at the sky. Where was the one who had encouraged me to draw, who loved me the most?

After our walk, Susan encouraged my father to take us out to lunch. He didn't fight her, even though we almost never ate out. We had a late lunch at the Bluebird Inn, across the street from the Little League field where my mother had met Paul Sullivan in the bleachers. As I often did when I was reminded of her, I wondered if I'd see her again one day.

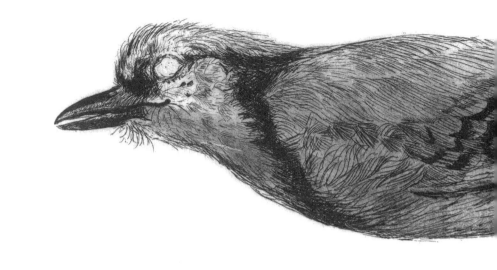

$23.$ *The night after our walk in the bird sanctuary,* the phone rang. When I answered, the woman on the other line said hello and then hung up.

At first I thought it was one of my father's relatives from Brazil, who would call once or twice a year, to wish him a happy birthday or something. This voice had an accent like my dad's relatives, so the first few times I called for him to pick up the phone. Every time the line went dead.

Once a week, at least, the call came. I almost always answered the phone. Every time I picked it up now, I expected the voice.

"Hello," it would say. And then there would be a very long silence. I would hold the phone at my ear, imagining who was in that empty space, the fuzz that could have been waves on the ocean, or just white noise.

I wouldn't have paid so much attention to the calls if I hadn't thought it might be my mother. But the woman's voice sounded so foreign, like she was calling from another country. The accent. My mom didn't have an accent.

I was at the supermarket with my dad one day, standing at the checkout counter. He was counting change in his hands. The woman ringing up the groceries asked my dad where his accent was from. He told her he was born in Brazil. Just then I remembered being in the same exact place, but when I was younger—years before, with my mother. I could hear her voice as if she were there, counting change in the checkout line at the supermarket. And the same exact thing had happened—the checkout woman had asked my mother where her accent was from. "I'm Czech," she had said.

Accent? I had forgotten.

I'd never noticed my mom's accent. Even when

people pointed it out, I didn't hear it. But now I knew why that oddly familiar voice saying hello on the other end of the phone sounded foreign. My mother did have an accent, but I'd always been too close to recognize it. More than two and a half years had passed since I'd heard her voice.

For months the prank calls were soothing, but then I became frustrated. I wanted the voice to say more than hello, but it didn't.

24. *In all, three years passed from the time I'd* last seen my mother to when I saw her again.

It was a spring day, very much like the one when she had first announced she was leaving, when I spotted her walking across the playing fields at school, hand in hand with a young girl.

I could hardly believe what I was seeing. She turned and looked at me. My mother, like a deer in the woods, staring. And just like a deer, she bounded off without a word.

My father was waiting for me after practice. I was hysterical. I couldn't breathe or talk.

I want to tie her to a stake and burn her!

"Breathe, Jeremy," I remember Dad saying. "What happened?"

"I saw her. I saw her. She looked at me. She didn't know me. She was with a girl. She stopped and looked and walked away."

"Who, Jeremy? Who?"

"My mother! The devil!"

"Calm down, Jeremy, calm down. Don't talk like that."

"Take me home. You're going to call her. Tell her what she's doing to me."

"Okay, Jeremy, okay."

When we got home, my father called her.

"Phoebe," he said, "it's Carl." I was stunned that it was that easy—just pick up the phone and call her. It was like he was calling heaven to ask God a favor. "Your son is here, and he's hysterical. He won't stop screaming. He said you saw him at school today and you walked the other way. No . . . I don't care . . . He won't stop screaming."

My head was throbbing from crying, when my dad handed me the phone. I wanted to die, but I was too mad.

"You!" I screamed at her. "You saw me and you walked away! How could you? You're a nightmare, a monster! You're going to see me. *Nobody* is going to stop me from seeing you."

"Okay, Jeremy," the voice said.

That voice.

And so, that Sunday, the three-year spell was broken.

She was due to come at noon. My father and Susan were away for the day. It was pouring rain. The rhododendrons were in bloom. She showed up a little after one thirty.

I watched her as she got out of the car and walked to the door, thin, blond, wearing a light dress and a raincoat. She rang the doorbell. I hid by the window, watching her.

Because she was late, I did not answer the door.

She returned to her car and waited for a few minutes with the engine running. Then she left.

• • •

That night she called the house and asked to speak with me.

"What would you like me to do, Jeremy?" she asked. I couldn't say anything.

When I was younger, my mother met people here and there, in the produce aisle at the supermarket—total strangers she would tell her life story, about how her mother had abandoned her as a child, put her in boarding schools in Prague where she was raised by strict nuns. People said she had an accent. I never heard it. But her voice sounded foreign now.

"I don't even know you."

"Jeremy?"

"Why didn't you stop? Why didn't you say anything when you saw me on the field?"

"I didn't recognize you," she said. "My vision is getting worse. I'm nearsighted. I didn't have my glasses."

"But I walked right up to you."

"You look different," she said.

"So you did see me!"

"No, I don't think I did."

"Then how can you say I look different?"

"Julie showed me pictures of you."

"I don't understand. How can you even call me your son, when you don't talk to me for three years, but yet you can spend time with a stranger's kids? You hold hands with that little girl, and then you look at your own son and you don't recognize him?"

"Jeremy," she said. "You don't know how much I think about you."

"How am I supposed to know that? You never see me! You see Julie. I know you do."

I hung up the phone.

She called back.

"What happened is in the past, Jeremy. We need to move forward."

"But why didn't you see me? Why didn't you call, or write?"

"Your father had had enough pain," she said. "He needed you more than I did. But now the timing's right, so God brought us together."

"Okay, okay," I said. "I don't want to hear any more! I can't listen to it."

"Jeremy, you are a talented boy," my mom said. "I want you to create the way you were meant to, to share your gifts with the world. You're going to change the world. I see it when I pray, in my dreams."

My mother and I set up a date a week later for her to pick me up. When she arrived, I walked out to the car, a small silver sportscar. I opened the passenger door and sat down in the seat without looking at her. She asked me what I wanted to do.

I wanted to go to the bait-and-tackle store to get some lures.

She drove down the road. I looked at her now, her face looked pale and her eyes were icy blue. It was a little cold and she was wearing leather gloves. She put her hand on my knee and then put it back on the wheel.

"The week before you were born," she said "we were sitting by the window in the kitchen. A robin had made a nest in the butterfly bush, and soon there were two little chicks in it. Every time the mommy came to feed the chicks, they stuck their heads up and started chirping: *peep, peep, peep.* And every time they chirped, you gave a big kick in my belly, and my breasts leaked milk all over my dress. The birdies were talking to you. 'Come fly with us,' they said. 'Be free.'"

"Why are you telling me this?" I asked her.

"Because Jeremy, you're different."

We drove on to the bait and tackle store and little more was said.

On later visits I expected her to express her regret for what she'd done, apologize for leaving. But she never did.

We talked about things at school. She taught classes in another town.

"The kids can't sit still," she said. "I feel like a baby-sitter." She laughed. "Years ago it wasn't like this. I think it's the broken family. None of the kids have parents. I call home to complain—'Bobby isn't doing his homework'—and I talk to a brother or sister."

I was stunned that she couldn't see that she herself had broken a family.

My mom started to call me up when her husband was late coming home from work. We'd talk about things, and then as soon as Paul walked in the door, my mom would hang up.

"Paul's still not home yet," my mom said when I picked up the phone. "Oh, someone's on the other line. Maybe it's him." She didn't ask if I could hold. I just heard a click. I waited for a few seconds, then hung up. A few minutes later she called back.

"He still hasn't called."

"That wasn't him?"

"No."

She was crying. Her voice quavered; her words were slurred. She sounded drunk. I felt like I had sitting at the dinner table with my dad in the weeks after my mom left, listening to him tell me how he was going to kill her, or himself.

"Mom, it's okay. He'll be home soon."

"What if he got in a car accident?"

"I'm sure he's fine."

"Yeah, you're right," she paused. "You know, Jeremy, you and I have been on this earth several times together in past lives. We've always been close; I've had dreams about it. But in the next life, you'll be alone, because I can barely finish this one. I'm tired, Jeremy. I'm fed up. I've lived on this earth long enough. I'm ready to go."

"Ready to go? What does that mean?"

"It means I'm tired, Jeremy."

"Don't talk like that."

I heard a long breath on the other side.

"Jeremy," she said, crying. "You're more important to me than anyone on this earth. You never stopped being important to me."

"Good," I said, a little frustrated. "Well, don't worry. I have to go. He'll be home soon."

"The last thing I want is to be a burden on my children."

"You're not a burden—don't talk silly. Things will be fine."

But I didn't understand. If I was so important to her, how could she have left me for so long?

"Destiny" was my mom's favorite word. I was "destined" to be an artist; she was "destined" to leave her two children. She told me that we choose our parents before we're born.

Does that mean I chose all of this?

But I knew she felt guilty for having left. She said she sometimes woke in the middle of the night screaming. Paul would ask her, "What's wrong? What's wrong?" She said she didn't know.

One night she called, and I knew immediately that she was alone and drinking. Her voice had that high and very emotional tone I now knew came from too much wine. It was my thirteenth birthday. She started the conversation by singing "Happy Birthday."

"It's five forty p.m." she said. "That's the time that you were born. You are my baby boy. . . ." At this point she broke down. "I want to wish you a very, very, veerrryy happy birthday. I want to tell you that I love you so much, and that you're going to be famous. I'm sorry, I'm sorrryyy for everything I've ever done to you. You are . . . I'm so proud of you. I'm messed up. I know I'm messed up."

"Mom," I interrupted. "Stop, it's okay."

"But you're the best thing . . . I'm going to get better. I'm a good person; I'm a very strong person. I never meant to hurt you. I will resolve this . . . I will."

25. A few days later I was sitting by the picture window in Julie's room, staring out at the large apple tree at the back of our yard, when the phone rang.

"Hello?"

"It's me," Julie said. She was calling from her college dorm room in Rhode Island.

"What's up? You don't sound good."

"You seen Mom lately?"

"No. Not for a week or so."

"Talked to her?"

"She called to wish me a happy birthday."

"How did she sound?"

"Drunk and emotional, but that's nothing new."

"I'm worried. Things aren't going well with Paul. She thinks he's seeing another woman."

"Hmm." I was staring out at the big apple tree at the back of our yard. The old wood bench, where my dad went to cry when he was in his deepest despair, was rotting and barely showed through the brambles by the edge of the woods.

"You should call her, Jeremy."

"And say what?"

"Just say hi. She's not doing well."

"Hmm."

"Is that all you can say? 'Hmm'?"

"What am I supposed to say? That she . . ."

My sister read my mind. "You're above that, Jeremy."

"Am I?"

"Call it karma."

"Karma?"

"It's what you were going to say, that she got what she deserves."

"But I'm above that."

"Yes," Julie said. "This is serious. Mom's in trouble. Call her."

"Okay. I'll call her."

"And call me back to let me know what she says."

I hung up with Julie and dialed my mom's number.

"Hi, it's Paul and Phoebe. Leave a message."

I hung up and called Julie back.

"She's not there. I got the answering machine."

"That's not good."

"I'd go over if I could, but I can't drive."

"I'm coming home," Julie said. "Soon."

"It's that bad?"

"I'm afraid it might be."

The next morning, Julie pulled up in the driveway. She was smoking a cigarette, but put it out before she walked into the kitchen. I was sitting at the kitchen table eating a bowl of cereal.

"Hey, Julie. You're home."

"I guess so," she said, putting her car keys down on the kitchen counter. "Did you ever get a hold of Mom?"

"No," I said. "Why?"

Julie sighed. She paced up and down the room.

She was wearing a baseball cap. I knew Julie meant business when she wore a cap.

"Paul left her last night. She took some pills. A friend of hers found her passed out in their apartment this morning. They had to pump her stomach, and still . . ."

"What? Where is she?" My heart started to beat faster.

"She's at Bridgeport Hospital."

"Is she okay?"

"She's alive."

"Are they letting her out?"

"No. They're going to keep her there. The doctor said for a while."

"What's wrong with her?"

"She's depressed, Jeremy. For God's sake! When are you going to grow up? She tried to kill herself. She's borderline."

"Okay, okay, Julie. Don't get mad at me. Borderline what?"

"Borderline." Julie touched her head, hard, with her index finger. "You know, Jeremy, she's not stable."

"What does that mean?"

"It means she needs us now more than ever."

I'd made plans to go fishing with Stephen, but I knew I wasn't going to enjoy it. "It's not all about you!" I could hear Julie say. *But it's my life, isn't it?* I was thinking about my mom. *All the things she pulled, and I'm supposed to wipe it clean, pretend it never happened?* What about all the times I needed her? I could have been cruel and ignored her problems. I could have even said a few mean things. But I would rise above and be mature.

She needs our love and support. But she had that before, and it wasn't enough. Will it be enough now, or will she try to do it again?

"Where do you want to go fishing?" Stephen asked. "I caught some big bass at the reservoir last night."

"Nah."

"How about Grady's Pond?"

"Nah."

"Well you tell me then."

"Why don't we just fish in your pond?"

It was a warm day, but the air was cool, and big cottony clouds drifted by. Natalie made us sandwiches, and we ate out on the porch.

"Why aren't you eating, honey?" Natalie asked me.

"I'm not so hungry."

"That's not the Jeremy I know," Stephen said, pretending he was talking in his mom's voice.

"Oh, Stephen," she said. "Maybe I spoiled you too much." And she went inside the house.

"Mothers," Stephen said.

"Yeah," I said.

I took my plate in and left it by the sink. Stephen left his on the table outside.

"Oh, leave that," Stephen said. "Natalie will take care of it."

We walked down to the pond with our fishing rods.

I took my first cast and snagged my lure on something.

"What the hell!" I yelled. "My first cast, and I get . . ."

"You must be snagged on the tree down there," Stephen said. "Some day I'm going to dive in there with a snorkel and grab all the lures I've lost on that thing."

I thought of the tree down there, fallen and submerged, covered with all our tackle. *If only we could go back and pick up all the lures we lost.* I pulled hard and snapped the line.

I lay down in the grass near the big weeping willow and stared up at the sky.

"What's wrong?" Stephen asked. "Something's wrong. I can tell."

"Nothing," I said.

Three vultures circled above us.

"Remember when we used to lie out in the field and pretend we were dead?" I asked. "We hoped the vultures would land in the field."

"Yeah," Stephen said.

"Never worked, did it?" I asked.

"Because we don't smell dead." Stephen said.

"Next time we'll rub some roadkill on our shirts."

"Maybe that's it," I said.

Stephen cast a few more times.

"Aren't you going to fish?" he asked.

"I don't feel like it. My mom's in the hospital."

"I knew it. What happened?"

"She kind of . . . hurt herself."

"You going to go see her?"

"It's too nice a day to be in a hospital. I'd rather just hang out, you know?"

"Do you want to stay over tonight?"

"I don't know if I should. Julie's back from college. And my mom . . . you know."

Stephen hooked some weeds with his lure. "Is she in bad shape?"

"She took a bunch of pills. She tried to kill herself."

As they came from my mouth, the words rang true, and I was in shock.

"Oh," Stephen said, "she tried to check out?"

"I guess so."

Stephen stopped reeling his lure. "Did she really?"

"That's what Julie said. She probably did it to get attention."

"Dude . . . that's pretty harsh."

"Harsh?" I said, throwing a stone in the pond. "That's just how I feel!"

Stephen cast in the pond again and pulled the lure back with some more weeds on it.

"Are you going to visit?" he asked.

"I'm trying to enjoy a nice day. I used to be able to. Why can't I? She's ruining it again. Why do I even care?"

"How bad is she? Maybe you should go see her today. I mean, if she dies, you might feel bad."

"I'm not going to run after her. That's the whole point. I'm not sure I can forgive her. Not today. Maybe another day." I looked up at the sky.

Maybe tomorrow.

26. *I couldn't sleep well, even in my own bed* at home. I wasn't very good at being stubborn and standing my ground. *I might feel better, I might be able to sleep, if I just forgive her.*

In the night I walked down to Julie's room. I knocked lightly on her door and poked my head in.

"Julie . . . ," I whispered.

"Jeremy?" she asked, half asleep.

"I don't want to bother you," I said. "But can we go see Mom in the morning? Will you take me?"

"Yes, Jeremy," she said. "Go back to bed."

I dreamed of my mom in a hospital bed, dressed in white clothes, with light pouring in through the window. A vase of flowers was on the table next to her. She looked like an angel.

In the morning Julie drove me to Bridgeport Hospital to see my mom. I hadn't been to a hospital since I'd broken my wrist playing kickball in third grade. I walked up to the woman at the front desk.

"Who are you here to see?" she asked sweetly.

"Phoebe," I said.

"Full name please?" the woman asked.

"Phoebe Vrabec."

"There is no one here with that name."

I had to think for a minute. The woman looked at me, puzzled.

"Phoebe Sullivan."

"Yes," she said, "okay. Room 401."

I went to the fourth floor and down a long corridor as the woman described. I checked the door numbers one by one, my heart beating faster and faster the closer I got to 401.

There were a few coins jingling in my pocket. I silenced them with my hand. It was quiet and air-conditioned, and the lights were pure and white. The door to 401 was open.

I peeked in.

I saw my mom's feet at the end of the bed, then her small body and her head, her cheek resting on the pillow. Like in my dream, brilliant light poured in through the window, and my mom was dressed in white. There were flowers on her bedside table. But next to the vase was something I hadn't seen for a long time.

The *Book of Birds*.

My mom looked at me.

"Jeremy," she said, and a big smile spread across her face. I felt small, like her child, an infant. "You're looking at this?" she asked, and put her hand on the *Book of Birds*. "There was a time when I needed it."

The *Book of Birds* was from another time. It was like I hadn't even made it. It had all my paintings of birds up until the day my mom left.

She took it with her. She stole it.

"No," I said, "you can keep it. I made a new one."

My mother's hair was matted in the back. I could see when she lifted her head to hand me the book. The cardboard cover with its painting of the warbler was faded. It looked old, like it was from another century.

"I took it with me because it made me think of you," she said.

I reached out to take it.

"You may not think so," she continued, "but I thought about you every day."

Her eyes didn't look at me. They were bright blue, especially against her pale, pale skin.

"You did?"

"You didn't know how bad I felt?"

"How could I know?"

"Because you know me," she said. "We've spent several lives together. You couldn't be the knowing person you are if you didn't have several lives behind you. And this is not our last life together, our story is not over."

As I looked at my mom, moments from the last

years flashed through my mind. *The pain she caused. She could have seen me if she wanted to.*

"There is a bird that the king of Austria kept in a cage," my mom began again. "The bird had the most beautiful voice of any in the world. But before that bird could sing to its full potential, its eyes had to be pierced. That bird is you, Jeremy. You were blinded when I left you. You were hurt beyond any hurt you'd ever felt. But you went into your soul to find yourself, and miracles happened."

I didn't know what to say. The words were soothing, like things she used to tell me to make me feel special, but the story felt crafted to make her feel better more than me.

But was there truth to it all?

As I turned the pages of the old *Book of Birds*, I thought, *Maybe she's right.* My drawings were so much better now. I felt like I saw things more clearly. I was embarrassed by these drawings.

"I'm your mother," she said. "There are things I know about you that you don't even know yet."

"Like what?"

"Like you are a powerful creator. Julie told me that you helped your uncle build a wall. She said you became stronger. You know, each stone you lifted was a trial. You carried each stone and found a place for it, and at the end you made something more beautiful than even you could have imagined. You surprised yourself. Am I right?"

"Yes."

"You know," she said, holding my *Book of Birds* again. "Without this I could not have left. I saw it one day in your bedroom and I was in awe. I was so miserable, Jeremy—you could not imagine. I grew up being told that I was stupid, that I wasn't good at anything. I saw the book and all the colorful birds, and it gave me strength. It gave me hope to turn the pages. That I had made such a beautiful boy capable of such miracles! I knew you didn't need me. There was no other way out. You see? In a strange way I felt like I never left you. You were with me through your paintings."

"That doesn't make sense," I said.

"No, no," she said, "it does. It may be hard to understand now, and it is, but you'll understand one day. When you have no choice, you're sometimes better off . . . I felt like there wasn't any place for me. That's how I ended up here. I told myself I was finished with life on earth. I didn't want to live. But now I feel God wants me here. I think my purpose now is to help you make your dreams come true. I love you, Jeremy."

I leaned over her bed and gave my mom a hug. I started crying on her shoulder. "I love you, Mom," I said.

"I'm alive for you, Jeremy. No one will ever come between us again."

"I hope not," I said.

I knew my mom was crazy, and she was sometimes wrong. But she wasn't wrong all the time. It felt sometimes like we were standing on two distant mountains with a bottomless canyon between us. I could shout as loud as I wanted, and my words seemed to get lost in a cloud of misunderstanding. She could talk and talk, and not a word would make sense. There was no way of crossing the canyon, but at times the clouds cleared, and in that moment it seemed that God, or someone like God, was speaking through her, and her words were so crisp and clear I felt like I could touch them. She told me I was going to be an artist. She said things happen for a reason and make us stronger.

I hope she's right.

Acknowledgments

Many thanks to Elaine Bleakney, Kevin Dunn, Sam Messer, Elaine Markson, Emily Meehan, and Lizzy Bromley. Thanks also to Sarah Stabile for her insights and support through numerous revisions. Most of all, thank you Rick Richter, for teasing this book into being.